DETOUR TO HARMONY

DETOUR TO HARMONY

MEGAN SQUIRES

May all of life's detours lead you on the road to happiness.

CHAPTER ONE

*T*hese were Miles Callahan's final minutes of stardom, and he couldn't wait for them to be over.

Years ago, the crescendo of cheers ringing throughout the arena as he thrummed the last notes on his guitar would've energized him. He would have buzzed with that same anticipation, and the insistent chants demanding an encore would've been met with glad agreement.

Performing had been Miles' passion, his purpose and ultimate dream in life.

Right now, his life's purpose sat cross-legged on the tour bus floor, likely with a plate full of dinosaur nuggets in his lap and a bedtime story waiting to be cracked open resting upon the nightstand.

Miles couldn't get through the set fast enough.

But Lana had other plans and despite their

manager repeatedly instructing them to be out of the venue by ten, she egged the fans on.

"Oh, what's that?" Sauntering across the stage like a model on the catwalk, she cupped her manicured hand around the shell of her ear. "Y'all want one more?" The voice he had fallen in love with—the one that hit all the right notes and knew all the right things to say—now struck his nerves like an out of tune six string. "I think we can arrange that. What do you say, Miles?"

She turned on the heel of her pristine, white cowboy boot to meet his eye, if only to play things up for the crowd. Miles knew full-well Lana would do whatever she pleased whether or not he agreed to it. He was just along for the ride.

But that ride ended tonight.

They would finish this last leg of the tour, and contractually, he didn't owe her more than that. Still, he wondered if his plans were rash. Few people gave up on a career that had just gotten wings. Timber Rose had the potential to soar to the top of the billboards if their momentum kept moving along the same trajectory it had been these last few months.

But none of that mattered to Miles. Seeing his name in lights, on the charts, or even on an album cover wasn't a rush anymore.

Seeing his four-year-old son, Cooper, light up every time Miles came back from a gig or home from a venue—that's what fed his soul.

It took everything in him to go along with Lana's

little stunt. Knowing it would be the last time he'd need to made all the difference. Miles plucked his guitar pick from his mouth and ran it over the strings. It was a single chord, but the audience erupted in cheerful recognition.

"Looks like y'all know this one!" Lana crooned into the microphone. They ate it all up—her manufactured accent, her false enthusiasm. He had once, too, but he knew better now.

He played the song by rote. Despite the persistent requests and shouts for another track, the band exited the stage with the audience still cheering in expectance.

"Always good to leave them wanting more," their drummer said as he bounded offstage and traded his drum sticks for a towel. He swiped the rag over his brow, then ran it along the back of his neck where his shaggy hair met the edge of his collar. "You both have perfected that art."

Miles couldn't disagree. He did want more from Lana. He wanted her involvement in their son's life. He'd settle for the public acknowledgment that she even had a son, but that was a wish he wouldn't place any real stock in.

"Let's do this again soon, boys. It was fun," Lana said cloyingly before heading toward her dressing room, a multitude of journalists and cameramen hot on her heels. Their backstage pass placards swung around their necks like the tags on an obedient dog.

Miles didn't get his own dressing room. It had

originally been a battle to even get a seat on the band's tour bus. But his bandmates quickly discovered bunking with a four-year-old threw a monkey wrench in the wild, carefree road trip they'd envisioned. So the label splurged on a separate housing solution for Miles. It wasn't extravagant, and it didn't have all the bells and whistles their official bus boasted, but the trailer had plenty of room for Cooper to feel comfortable and that was all they needed.

"Hey buddy!" Miles shouted the moment he pushed open the door to their small home on wheels. "Did you miss me?"

The young boy abandoned his blanket and teddy bear and rushed toward Miles, all but slamming into his legs as he wrapped his little arms around him tight.

"Daddy!" Cooper rubbed his tired eyes on Miles' pant leg. "You're back!"

"How'd he do?" Moving down the aisle with his son clinging to him like a baby koala, Miles edged closer to his sister, Maddie. "Sorry we went longer than promised."

"Always do." Maddie shut Cooper's bedtime book and placed it on the cushion beside her.

"I know. I'm sorry. Lana did another song, even though we were explicitly instructed not to."

"It's not a problem, Miles. Promise. You know I love spending time with this little guy." Maddie moved her fist over Cooper's mop of hair, making it stand on end with electricity. "Plus, I had to soak in all I could get. Are you really still planning to leave town tomorrow?"

Miles lowered his chin in a nod. "I am. I have to, Mad. I need some distance. From Lana. From the band."

"From music?" His sister's serious gaze challenged him.

"Maybe, yeah. A little."

"Daddy, I saw you playing the guitar on the TV with that pretty lady."

If his heart had been whole to begin with, it would've shattered into a thousand little shards at his son's words. Lana wasn't *Mommy* or *Mama*, or even *Mom*. She was a "pretty lady" who used her voice to entertain the fans she referred to as her family. The sad reality was that she'd never even sung her own son a lullaby. She had it all backward and had no intention of ever looking back. No intention of acknowledging her past and Cooper's place in it.

A child got in the way of the things most important to Lana: success, appeal, and stardom. Her decision to sign over her parental rights at birth hadn't been a difficult one. That was the worst part of it all. She'd handed over her duties as though transferring ownership of a vehicle.

"So listen, buddy." Miles hoisted Cooper up to his middle, and the boy wrapped his legs around his waist. "One more sleep on the bus and then we're going to get Daddy's truck and go on an adventure."

"An adventure?"

"Yep. Just you and me."

"What about Auntie Maddie?"

"I'll FaceTime you every night, Coop." Miles pretended not to see the sheen of tears glistening in his sister's eyes. If she started crying, he wouldn't be far behind and he didn't have the emotional where-withal for any of that tonight. "And I'll send letters too. Lots of them."

"Promise?" The boy stretched out and lifted his pinky finger.

Madeline hooked hers onto it. "Promise. Love you, Cooper Trooper."

"Love you too, Auntie Maddie."

Maddie's eyes moved toward her younger brother and she took a big breath like she was going to confess something important. She shook her head and instead blurted, "What am I going to do without you two rugrats to look after?"

She went in for a hug, sandwiching Cooper between them. The young boy erupted in a high-pitched fit of giggles.

"Hey now," Miles said. "You mean ru*grat*." He squeezed his son tightly.

"Nope, I meant plural." Though he knew she was teasing, there was undeniable truth in her statement.

Maddie had been there for Miles throughout his entire life. With a seven-year age gap between them, she'd always been more of a mother figure than a big sister. And when their own mother had passed away from cancer when Miles was just a freshman in high school, his sister moved back home from college and slipped into that maternal role.

Now, for the first time in all of his adult life, Miles would be on his own. It was equal parts exhilarating and terrifying.

"I'm proud of you, Miles," Maddie said, her tone softer now. "You're a good man. And a good father."

At times, he didn't feel like either, but this was the chance to prove those statements true.

The path he'd been on just wasn't working for them anymore. It was time for a detour.

CHAPTER TWO

"*C*an I get you a refill of decaf, Eugene?" Scarlett Harmony cradled the carafe in her hands, hovering it over the old man's empty mug.

"You know what? I think I'll take regular."

Scarlett made a real show of flipping her wrist over to glimpse the face of her watch. "You are aware it's already noon. That cup of caffeine will keep you up past sundown, my friend."

"That's the goal." Eugene's eyes twinkled with mirth, wiry brows wiggling up and down on his forehead like caterpillars inching up a stem. "Lottie is letting me take her out tonight. The high school play of *Peter Pan*. You have the chance to see it yet? Some of those youngins are mighty fine actors. Mighty fine."

"I haven't yet, but it's on my list." Scarlett clapped her friend on the back. "Let me go switch this out and bring you the leaded stuff."

"And one of those iced sugar cookies, if you've got 'em."

"You know I do. Coming right up."

The Campfire Café was humming, smack-dab in the throes of the lunchtime rush. It was a blessing to be this busy, but at times it felt like Scarlett couldn't stay on top of things. She was riding the waves of success, but at any moment, those very waves could wash over her and pull her under. She'd recently hired another server, but had yet to see any real relief. The young girl was still learning the ropes, which had already resulted in three broken plates, two switched meals, and a forgotten to-go order. And that was just today's shift.

In a quest to change out the coffee pots, Scarlett made her way to the kitchen and caught her newest employee taking a quiet moment by the walk-in refrigerator, back slumped against the stainless appliance, head clasped in her hands. The poor girl was minutes away from a panic attack and her pallor was so ruddy she nearly looked sunburnt.

"How you hanging in there, Katie?" Scarlett settled the pot onto the nearby counter and ventured a step closer.

"I just gave Mr. McGregory his sandwich with pickles." The teen's lip trembled as she spoke. She pinned it between her teeth to scold the tears of overwhelm that threatened to fall.

"That's nothing that can't be fixed," Scarlett

assured. "Just have Dominic make him up a new one without pickles. Problem solved."

"Mr. McGregory is *allergic* to pickles!" Katie's hand flew to her forehead. "I nearly killed the man!"

Scarlett took the girl by the shoulders. "First of all, take a big breath with me, okay?" She inhaled so fully her lungs nearly ached, then hissed the breath out between her lips. Like an unspoken game of Simon Says, Katie did the same. "One more, okay?"

They repeated the calming exercise and Scarlett said, "Mr. McGregory isn't allergic to pickles. And tomorrow when he orders a BLT on rye and tells you he's allergic to tomatoes, don't believe that either. He's got it in his head that the only way to make sure his order isn't wrong is to blame his overwhelming pickiness on food allergies."

"He's not going to die? I think he ate an entire pickle slice before he realized they were on there."

"I mean, someday, sure. But not today. And certainly not because you accidentally put a pickle on his turkey club."

Eyes closed, Katie drew in another intentionally full breath, this time completing the soothing exercise all on her own. Relief eased into her features and calm crept back into her voice. "Thank you, Scarlett."

"Sure thing. Anytime. Listen, why don't you call it a day?" Scarlett suggested with a soft smile. She released Katie's shoulders. "I've got things handled here, and you're doing great with your training. You deserve to have the afternoon off."

"Are you sure? I don't want you to think I don't want to be here, because I do. I really love working for you and I love the Café. This place has always meant so much to me." The girl let a silent moment take the place of her words. "But don't you ever get over-whelmed?"

"Of course I do. Every day. Dealing with the public is a challenge; there's no denying that. Throw in a *hungry* customer and that only makes things more complicated. But I love feeding people. There's some-thing satisfying about providing a meal for a friend or a customer. Breaking bread together and all of that. It's what my father loved so much about this place." Oversharing as she often had a tendency to, Scarlett switched gears. "So tell me the tables you were working."

"I had eight, nine, and fourteen. Fourteen is the only one still waiting on their food. A young dad and his son. Dominic's just finishing up their order, I think."

Scarlett wiped her hands on the front of her half apron and nodded. "Got it. Considered them covered. You go home, get some rest, and I'll see you back here tomorrow."

Katie's two tables were already mid-meal, so Scar-lett refilled their drinks and left them to it. Mr. McGregory appeared satisfied with Scarlett's apology over the pickle debacle. The offer of a free slice of cheesecake upped that satisfaction to downright delight. She shouldn't make a habit of mollifying disgruntled customers with sweet treats, but Mr. McGregory was the editor of the *Harmony Ridge Gazette*, and he typically made his opinions known in print format for all to see. She didn't need their restaurant splashed over the pages of the newspaper, nor did she desire any bad press. Preventing a mess was always better—and often easier—than cleaning one up.

Just as she was topping off the water glasses at table nine, Dominic's hand came down on the bell at the pickup counter. "Order up!" his baritone voice boomed across the Café.

Scarlett rushed over. "Is this for table fourteen?"

Dom nodded the answer, and Scarlett grabbed the two plates, plus a hefty stack of napkins. The Peanut Butter and Honey Ants on a Log off the kid's menu was a notoriously sticky mess, although it was one of her favorites. Crunching into a piece of celery decorated with edible insects was a transportation device if ever food could be one. It swooped her right up and deposited her straight back into childhood, when meals were creative and food was fun.

Grateful her father had kept it on the menu all of these years, Scarlett's heart compressed around the nostalgia. Smiling to herself, she pulled a coloring book and a packet of crayons out from behind the cash wrap station and wove her way through the restaurant toward the only table still awaiting their food.

"I've got an Ants on a Log and a meatloaf." She

placed the kid's meal down in front of the man, along with the crayons and coloring book, then settled the meatloaf in front of the young boy. Just like she'd hoped, the child let out a big belly laugh.

"That's not for me. That's Daddy's!"

"Oh!" Scarlett swapped the plates dramatically, then rolled her eyes. "Silly me. So sorry about that."

Though the man didn't laugh in the boisterous way his young son had, Scarlett noted a flicker of amusement challenge the corners of his mouth. His eyes—had they not looked so desperately tired—showed an appreciation for her silly joke. Exactly what she'd been going for.

"Can I get you two anything else?" She clamped her hands to her legs to brush her palms against her apron.

The man slid the coloring book toward his son. "Maybe another pack of crayons?"

"Sure thing. I can bring you your own coloring book too, if you like," she offered, completely serious. "I've got a whole bunch of them."

"You don't need to do that," he said. "I can just tear out a few pages."

Well, if that wasn't the most endearing thing ever. "Sounds good. I'll grab those crayons and check back on you two in a few to see if there's anything else you need."

She tended to the other tables, but found her gaze persistently moving back toward the young father and son in the corner of the Café. The boy perched up on his haunches with his legs crossed beneath him, stretching over the table to steal the colors he needed from his dad. They would laugh every once in a while and the way the man looked at his son was full of a tender warmth Scarlett could tangibly feel, even though the look wasn't directed at her. Some sort of joy-filled osmosis reached into her heart and squeezed it tight.

She forced her gaze away and moved about the Café, aware of her intrusion.

After she'd made her rounds, Scarlett slid into the other side of Eugene's booth. "Your meal has been taken care of by another customer today, my friend."

Eugene had fallen on hard times as of late. It wasn't public knowledge, but Scarlett had seen the man scrape together his balance in nickels and dimes, and that just didn't sit well with her. When her father ran the Campfire Café, his motto to his customers had always been, "Pay what you can." Somehow, things always worked out in the end—the restaurant doors stayed open and the lights remained on, even after all these years of his generous sacrifice.

"Someone's covered my meal? Well, that's awfully nice of them," Eugene acknowledged, a little wink tacked on at the end. Scarlett knew she hadn't fooled him, but that would never stop her from trying. "Listen, I've got three extra tickets for that *Peter Pan* play tonight." With a shaky hand, Eugene slipped it into his worn-out billfold, then held the tickets out for Scarlett to take. "See if your brother and that new sister-in-law of yours want to go with you. I'd hate for the seats to go to waste."

Whether or not she would end up using them, Scarlett took the tickets all the same. It was Eugene's way of reciprocating her generosity, and that wasn't something she could turn down.

"You sure you don't need them?"

"Nope, just need one for me and one for Lottie. But the seats are next to ours and I'm planning to hold her hand tonight. So if the thought of an old couple canoodling makes you uncomfortable, might want to see if you can switch them out."

"Eugene!" Scarlett stood from the booth and playfully swatted him with the dishtowel draped over her shoulder. "Hand holding?" She covered her mouth in pretend shock. "So scandalous."

Eugene smiled to himself, all giddy and full of mischief.

"I'll see you tonight. And I'll see if I can find a good home for the other tickets."

She hugged Eugene goodbye before the old man shuffled out the door, then made her way about the Café once more.

Slowly approaching the father and son, she noticed the man's gaze focused wistfully out the window, taking in Harmony Ridge Row with its downtown shops and busy patrons running errands and exchanging pleasantries. The boy colored furiously in the book, paying no heed to lines and boxes. That was Scarlett's kind of artist.

"That's some great work there…" She paused, as though searching for the young child's name.

"I'm Cooper." He surprised her when he reached out his little hand for a shake. Someone had taught the boy his manners. His mature behavior was down-right adorable. "What's your name?"

"Scarlett."

"That's a pretty name." Cooper's tongue popped out of his mouth while he redirected his focus back to the coloring book. "My dad's name is Miles."

Scarlett's attention blinked over to the boy's father, his handsome looks drawing a ragged breath from her. He had tousled hair the color of dark cocoa, blue lagoon eyes a woman could sink into and never resur-face from, and a square jaw that was the very defini-tion of masculinity. He was the sort of handsome that made you forget exactly what you were supposed to be doing—like running a restaurant in the middle of the lunch hour rush. Scarlett collected herself. "Nice to meet you both."

"Likewise." Miles' eyes sparked a little when they met her own, and she felt a flutter in her stomach that took her by surprise. A smile lifted the corner of his mouth when he asked, "Is there anything to do around here tonight?" He slid his gaze toward his son. "Kid-friendly."

"Believe it or not, there's a play at the high school just down the road. *Peter Pan.*"

"*Peter Pan*! I love *Peter Pan*!" Cooper shrieked.

"Is something like that usually sold out the day

of?" She could see Miles trying to temper the boy's enthusiasm, but not much could be done there. He'd already picked up his fork to use as a hook and his voice switched to pirate talk with lots of *rrr's* and throaty noises.

"Usually, but I just so happen to have two extra tickets." She withdrew them from the pocket of her apron and placed them on the table. "You'll have to sit with me and my friends Eugene and Lottie, but we're good company."

Miles moved for his billfold.

"Nope. They were a gift to me, so I won't take anything for them." She waved him off.

She could tell he was reluctant to do so, but he lifted his hips to slide his wallet back into place. "Can we at least pick you up then? Something to reciprocate your kindness?"

Scarlett had her own mode of transportation, but just like she'd done earlier with Eugene, she chose to accept Miles' offer of payment. Kind gestures were worth their weight in gold these days. "That would be great. I get off work around five, so if you can swing by here around five-thirty, I should be ready."

"We'll meet you here then." Miles trapped her gaze with his for a moment, then looked across the table at his son. "Did you hear that, buddy? After we go to the park and drop our stuff off at the Inn, we'll come back here to pick up Scarlett and go to the play."

"Yup." Cooper snapped a piece of celery between his front teeth. "I heard."

"Okay." Miles laughed softly. "Thank you, Scarlett. This means a lot."

"Oh, it's nothing," she said noncommittally, but the look of sincere appreciation he gave her made her question those words.

"It's not nothing," he said, shrugging. "I mean it. Thank you. We'll see you tonight."

CHAPTER THREE

*M*iles had driven until the gauge hovered right over *E* and threatened to dip into the red. That had been his plan. A prayer and five tanks of gas to see how far they could get on this first stretch of the journey.

The old, single cab truck had always been a clunker, but it really showed its age as it coughed its way up the hills and struggled into higher and more mountainous elevations. He knew the run-down vehicle needed a break, and by the looks of Cooper slumbering in his booster seat next to him, Miles figured they could all benefit from a rest.

Harmony Ridge.

The town's sign had been anything but extravagant—just a name and population number—but there was a comfort rooted in its unassuming simplicity.

Maybe it was the name that drew him in. Miles

had been searching for some semblance of harmony in his life longer than he could remember. Funny, one would think being in a band would foster that, what with making music on a daily basis and all. But the music of his soul had been so out of rhythm that nothing felt harmonious, least of all his daily existence.

His GPS had directed him to the town's gas station, an internet search to an overnight booking at the local inn, and his growling stomach led him into the Campfire Café. Things finally felt in sync and he was grateful for the simple sense of stability in a new town with new people and new places.

Anytime Miles would question the sanity of his plan—this clean break from his former life and voca-tion—he just looked at Cooper. That precious boy was Miles' true reason for leaving. For getting as far from Nashville as he could. For pulling out of the music industry in search of a place to sink down new roots for them both.

Kindergarten would start in the fall, and then Cooper would really need some daily consistency. A makeshift tour bus and a sporadic concert schedule couldn't provide that.

But Miles did have a little time to explore their options before enrolling Cooper in school. Harmony Ridge felt as good a place as any to start that journey.

The people were kind and gracious, that small town hospitality evident from the get-go.

He had no illusions that their first real stop would

be their final destination, but they would enjoy whatever time they had here.

Plus, Cooper hadn't stopped talking about *Peter Pan* ever since Scarlett invited them to tag along to the play.

"Do you think Tinker Bell will actually fly?"

Miles stood behind Cooper as they took in their reflections in the bathroom mirror. He tightened the small knot at the top of his son's tie and ran a comb through his just-washed hair. The park they'd visited that afternoon had been a good one, with big slides and a fast merry-go-round and loads and loads of sand, much of which ended up in Cooper's shoes and sprinkled throughout his curly brown strands.

"And is she going to be teeny-teeny-tiny?" The little boy squished his thumb and index finger together to indicate a small space. "Or will she be people-sized?"

"My guess is people-sized."

Cooper hopped down from the stool and rushed into the bedroom they'd rented at the Inn. He flung open his suitcase to pull his beloved teddy bear from the zippered pouch. "Can Orson come with us?"

He was at the age that Miles should probably start discouraging the bear as a constant companion, but with so much of Cooper's life in flux right now, Miles figured it best to allow the toy to tag along. Comforts came in all forms, and a beloved stuffed animal was harmless in the long run.

"Orson can absolutely come with us. But he's not

dressed for the occasion." Miles ran the zipper around his own luggage and pulled out a houndstooth bowtie, the one he often wore for media engagements or photo shoots. While Lana had always been extravagant with her leather and lace, the guys in the band weren't often as gussied up. Their usual uniform comprised blue jeans, boots, and a button up flannel shirt—your standard attire for cowboys and the musicians who played the tunes cowboys listened to.

Miles took the bowtie and secured it around the teddy bear's tattered neck, then handed him back to Cooper. "Now he's ready for a night at the *theatre*." He said the last word in a fancy accent and it got the laugh out of Cooper he'd hoped for.

"Silly Daddy." Cooper jammed the animal under his arm and reached up for Miles' hand. "All set. Let's go get Miss Scarlett."

The clock on the wall indicated it was just a quarter past five. The Café was a short drive from The Inn on Harmony Lane, their temporary home for the next few days. He knew it wasn't a date—of course it wasn't—but he felt the altogether foreign sensation of nerves slide through his stomach. Other than Lana, he rarely spent time with women. And Scarlett was beautiful. There was no question about that, the kind of natural beauty that made you skid to a stop in your tracks.

Still, he wouldn't let his head venture into territory relating to attraction, or worse yet, relationships. She had been kind enough to invite them along and there wasn't anymore to it than that.

They left the Inn and Miles buckled his son and Orson into their seat, pulling the lap belt tightly across their middles. With a spring in his step he hadn't had in years, Miles rounded the back of the old truck and joined them in the cab. "Any special requests?" His fingers found the radio dial.

"Johnny Cash."

"Johnny Cash it is." The two crooned to "Walk the Line" and only when he pulled up to the curb of the Café and glimpsed Scarlett waiting for them did Miles turn down the music.

He loved that his young son respected the country greats. He'd done his best to instill that appreciation from a young age, but he also knew sometimes you were just born with it. Old souls tended to gravitate toward the classics. That had certainly been the case for Miles back in his youth.

"There's Scarlett!" Cooper thrust his pointer finger into the air.

"Yep, I see her." Angling his vehicle up close to the sidewalk, Miles let it idle when he stepped out to greet their new friend. "Evening, Scarlett."

"Hi, Miles." Her smile was joy and light, and it affected every feature on her beautiful face. "You boys like to listen to your music pretty loud, huh?"

"Oh, just a little."

"I could hear you coming up the street before I

could see you." Miles would've felt self-conscious had she not quickly added, "Just the way I like it."

He guided her around to the passenger side of the vehicle, his hand gently on her elbow, and only then did he realize Cooper's booster was in the way. He'd have to move it to the middle of the bench seat to make room for the three of them in the cramped vehicle. "Hey buddy. Mind jumping out really quick so I can move your booster and Scarlett can sit here?"

"No, no, no." Scarlett shook her head. "I'll climb over."

"It's not a big deal to just move the seat." He felt dumb for not thinking to do all of this sooner.

"Nope. I can fit." She was already hoisting herself into the truck, shimmying past Cooper and Orson to plop into the middle seat of the cab.

Goodness, her easygoing nature was the biggest breath of fresh air. Apparently, he'd spent too much time with a certain woman who demanded her bottled water at a specific temperature and expected everyone to be at her beck and call, no matter the day, no matter the hour. Running with a diva for so long had a way of tainting women in general for Miles, yet Scarlett had already erased those preconceived notions. That had to be some sort of magic.

He returned to his position behind the wheel and angled back onto the two-lane road that led straight through the center of town. "You'll have to give me directions."

Scarlett nodded. "It's easy. Just a right up at the

four-way stop and then it'll be six blocks down on your left. You won't be able to miss it." Her eyes lowered to the dash. "What was that music you two were listening to before? Any artist I know?"

"Johnny Cash," Cooper said, fiddling with Orson's bowtie. "Everyone knows him."

"Yes, they do, and for good reason. He's an icon. You like country music, Cooper?"

"Yep. I sometimes like to listen to old stuff, but my favorite is Daddy's music."

Even though his gaze was directed out the windshield, Miles could feel Scarlett's eyes suddenly on him. "You play?"

"A little."

"Daddy is a guitar player for—"

"I used to play the guitar professionally," he quickly cut off his son. "But I'm looking to start something new."

"You know, the high school is looking for a new music teacher," she offered with a little shrug. "Not sure if that's your sort of thing."

"I've never taught. But we're not planning to stay in Harmony Ridge all that long."

"Ah. A pit stop on a bigger adventure?" It didn't come across as prying, and Miles was grateful for the conversation. It wasn't often that anyone showed interest in his plans. He almost didn't know what to do with that.

When they came to the stop, she indicated a right turn with her hand.

"Not really a pit stop, but a piece of the adventure," Miles replied to her earlier comment. He flicked his blinker on and made the turn.

It was easy to find the high school. All he had to do was follow the throng of cars clogging the lane as they waited their turn to pull into the lot ahead. He'd never seen so many people gathered for an after school event. The place where he grew up boasted at least four high schools, and while they had football games and dances and rallies, the local school wasn't the center of activity. Clearly, things were different in a small town.

"This is it," Scarlett said.

"All these people are here to see *Peter Pan*?" Cooper's eyes were wide as saucers. "Wow!"

"It's a supportive community." Scarlett unhooked her seatbelt after they'd parked in one of the last open spots and then moved to help Cooper with his. "One of the many things I love about Harmony Ridge."

"Have you lived here your whole life?" Miles took his key from the ignition.

"Yep," she said, then smirked when she added, "My full name is Scarlett Harmony."

"You *own* the town?" Cooper's voice jumped in octaves and in decibels, shooting clear into shouting territory.

"I don't own the town, but my family did start it. Many, many, many years ago." They all exited the vehicle together. "So I suppose I'm a little biased. But even if I didn't have such deep connections to this place, I think I'd still live here. It's got everything I need. Family, friends, and the best restaurant this side of the Ridge." Her lashes fluttered in a wink after that last comment, obviously referring to her café.

Miles wondered what it would feel like to be so settled. He'd been on the road since before Cooper was born. Home didn't refer to a specific place, but more of a feeling deep within when it was just the two of them. Home was fixing Cooper his favorite banana pancakes on a slow Sunday morning, tucking him into bed after a late night show, caring for him when he was sick. Home was the love he and his son shared, and that traveled with them like the lightest luggage wherever they went.

"Daddy, look! Brownies!"

With the thrill of a promised sugar rush, Cooper grabbed Miles by the hand and tugged him forward through the melee of high school students and parents cradling flower bouquets for their performers. Cooper was like a bloodhound, hot on the trail of the sugary scent. He came to a stop right in front of a folding table filled with an assortment of baked goods, a half dozen peppy cheerleaders perched behind the display.

"We're raising money for Nationals. Everything is buy one, get one free," a young girl rehearsed in her best saleswoman tone. "It's for a good cause," she added, as if the sweets needed any help selling themselves.

"It is, Daddy," Cooper pleaded. He pulled on Miles' pant leg. "It's 'cause I'm hungry."

Miles figured he could use the opportunity to teach his son about the importance of working hard for the things you wanted in life, just like the cheer squad was currently doing. Making plans and setting goals. Instead, he just handed over a ten-dollar bill and let Cooper make his selection.

There was such a weight to being a single parent. He constantly worried about the missed opportunities, about the teaching moments he was just too tired to follow through with.

But sometimes, a handful of saran-wrapped desserts was just a sweet treat, plain and simple. Not everything needed to be life-altering.

"Here, Miss Scarlett." Cooper lifted up an oatmeal cookie. "I got this one for you."

"That's so nice of you, Cooper." She made a big deal of the cookie. "How did you know this was my favorite?"

"I didn't." Cooper shrugged and snapped off a piece of his brownie between his front teeth. "But it's the one I don't like all that much, so I thought I would give it to you."

"Cooper," Miles scolded.

Scarlett lowered her eyes at Miles and shook her head. "Well, Cooper, then it's serendipity that it's my favorite, isn't it?"

"Seren-what?"

"Never mind, buddy." Miles guided his son by the shoulders to edge their way closer to the auditorium entrance. "Don't get that sticky goodness all over Orson."

"I won't," Cooper assured, but if his smudged mouth was any indication, it wouldn't be long before anything within a five-foot radius was dusted in powdered sugar or colorful sprinkles.

"It's kind of like pixie dust, isn't it?" Scarlett played along and Miles was completely in awe of her effortless ability to roll with all the punches that accompanied an evening with a four-year-old.

They moved up in line and finally had their tickets scanned by a student at the door.

"Do you need any help finding your seats?" the young man asked.

"Nope," Scarlett replied. "I know right where they are. Thanks, Jeremy."

Miles shouldn't have been surprised that Scarlett not only knew her way around the school's theatre but also happened to know the name of the kid working the door. The six degrees of separation seemed even fewer here, and that familiarity was a comfort.

"There they are!" Scarlett's hand shot up in a wave toward an older man and woman already in their seats about halfway down a row in the middle of the auditorium. "I found some friends to bring with me, Eugene."

They shimmied their way across the aisle, stepping around seated theatre patrons and avoiding the bags and purses that dotted the ground near their feet. The crowd was as impressive as any audience Timber

Rose had performed in front of. There was no denying that. It would kill Lana to know that a high school play could create just as much fanfare as one of their shows. He laughed a little at the thought.

"Good to meet you." Eugene stood and reached around Scarlett to shake Miles' hand, then Cooper's.

"I want to sit by the grandpa!" Cooper blurted, and before Miles had time for the proper amount of humiliation to form, Eugene said, "Good, because I want to sit next to the little tyke."

They all took their seats according to Cooper's request and Miles found himself on the end with Scarlett in between him and his son.

"You sure you don't want to switch?" He turned to face her. "He can get a little squirrelly. I don't want you to feel like you have to babysit him."

"Nope." She smiled. "This is perfect." She tapped Miles' knee reassuringly with her folded program. "Take the night off and just enjoy the magic that is our high school's performance of *Peter Pan*."

She had likely meant it to come across as somewhat satirical, but the evening truly was one of magic. Cooper squealed with delight when Tinker Bell did, in fact, fly over the stage, fluttering about as she sprinkled glitter over the cast and into the audience. He probably didn't notice the thin wires and pulleys that made it possible, simply because he chose to believe.

Maybe that's what Miles needed to do more of: choosing to believe in the magic all around them.

It was there in the way Eugene, Scarlett, and

Lottie welcomed them into the fold like they were old friends. It was in the way the cast seized the moment and created a perfect hour and a half, entertainment-filled escape for their viewers. And it was in the applause from the audience, as great and as loud as any packed concert or sold-out stadium.

Harmony Ridge was a town like no other, and it felt like providence—or maybe even a little of that serendipity Scarlett spoke of—that had led them there.

CHAPTER FOUR

Scarlett grabbed her purse from beneath the cash register and slung it onto her shoulder.

"I'm headed out for a couple of hours, Dom!" she hollered into the kitchen. "See you in a bit!"

Dominic flicked a salute, followed by a nod. She was grateful for such a dependable chef to run the culinary side of things at the restaurant. When her father had first passed and the responsibility of the Café fell into her lap, she thought she could do it all: cook, run the front of the house, organize the work schedules. As a teenager, she helped as a server and figured she knew the ins and outs of it all. She couldn't have been more wrong.

She was good at organizing and good with people. Not as great when it came to cooking, but in a pinch, she could make do. It was love at first culinary bite when her old friend, Dominic Hart, answered her ad in the *Gazette*. Their working relationship was perfection—a symbiotic partnership that made the Campfire Café run like a well-oiled machine.

Over the last year, she'd also taken on enough line cooks and additional servers to lift even more weight from her shoulders. Still, at the end of the day, she was fully aware it was her responsibility to live out her father's legacy. That wasn't transferrable, and she wore the responsibility like a beloved, hand-me-down heirloom.

Heading toward the door, she found her long-time server, Timmy, on her way to the exit. "I'll be back in a couple hours, right before the dinner crowd."

"Sounds good, Scarlett. I'll hold down the fort until then."

Tuesdays were easily her favorite day of the week, and she had her brother, Levi, to thank for that. He ran the Perfect Harmony Bakery a little jaunt further down Harmony Ridge Row, and that new endeavor demanded all of his attention. Prior to taking on a storefront, however, he was an avid volunteer at the local animal shelter. Weekly, he would read to the animals, a longstanding tradition that started one Fourth of July some five years ago. On that particularly noisy day of celebration, volunteers discovered that scared shelter animals benefited from the one-on-one attention. Storytime provided a semblance of peace and calm amid the commotion.

Levi had once asked Scarlett if she could cover a last-minute Tuesday volunteer shift. She loved it so much that she made it a standing appointment on her calendar.

But before she drove out to the Humane Society today, she needed to make a quick stopover at the library. Sure, she doubted the dogs and cats would notice if she reread last week's book once more, but she adhered to the motto that if you were going to do something, you might as well give it your all. The least she could do for these abandoned pups was read them a brand-new story. They deserved that and so much more.

Harmony Ridge Library was less than a half-mile from the Café, and firing up the engine to drive seemed silly, if not irresponsible. It was late spring and while the temperature was on a steady incline, it was still cool enough to take a brisk stroll down the street without working up a real sweat. She waved at Carl Manly as he slipped mail into her neighboring shop owners' boxes, and she smiled at each passerby she encountered, most of whom she knew, at least by name and more often through years of friendship.

By the time she got to the library, she could see it was crowded, the parking lot chock-full of minivans and SUVs. By the looks of it, there had been a story-time event for little ones that had recently wrapped up. Moms with wide strollers and stacks of board books congregated in the lobby, lining up play dates and exchanging phone numbers while their children used their tired bodies as jungle gyms. Scarlett moved past the congestion and pressed her way through the turnstile.

The children's section was something out of an amusement park, with large, climbable decorations that looked like they were taken straight from a fairy-tale. It was the sort of place a child would beg to visit, and that board books surrounded it was a huge bonus.

The shelves were shorter in this area of the building, making it easier for children to snag their favorite stories from the top. Crouching down, Scarlett scanned the colorful spines and tossed several new-to-her books into her canvas tote. Just as she was satisfied with her selection, she pressed up to her feet and her eyes locked with the most captivating blue ones she'd ever seen.

"Miles!" She leaned over the shelving unit to glimpse Cooper sitting cross-legged at his dad's feet, thumbing furiously through an illustrated book. "What are you two doing here?"

"Just finished up storytime and I promised Cooper we could check out a few books. But then I forgot the whole bit about needing a library card, so I told him he would have to just read these books quickly while we're here."

"Well, it's a good thing you ran into me because I just so happen to have a library card that is begging to be used."

Miles smiled appreciatively, a go-to look she'd come to expect from him. It was almost as though the man had never had any favors done for him. "You sure that's not asking too much?"

"You didn't ask, and no, it's not. I've got an entire stack of books to check out for myself." She hoisted the bag high so he could see her collection.

"Do you have a young reader in your family?" His brow pinched in the middle, an inquiring look buckling his features.

"Me? Oh, no! I read to dogs," she clarified, realizing that was no clarification at all. "On Tuesdays, I visit the animal shelter and read to the abandoned pets there. I figured I would freshen up my collection before I headed that way today." She paused, wondering if it was too presumptuous to ask the two to tag along. She decided to just go for it. "Would you guys like to come with me?"

Cooper popped up and peered over the shelving partition between them. "You read to doggies?" His eyes curved wide open. "Like in dog language?"

"No, in English. I tried to learn how to bark, but it didn't translate well."

Miles released a little laugh. "You really wouldn't mind if we tagged along?"

"I would prefer it, actually. I can always use some accountability to keep me from coming home with a new furry friend," she admitted. "It's a real struggle."

"Daddy says dogs are a big commit..." Cooper's tongue tangled over the long word. "Commitment."

"They really are. You need to feed them and walk them and love them——"

"And clean up their poopies!"

"Yes. All of those things. But the volunteers at the shelter take care of most of the messy stuff for these particular animals. We just get to love on them. Would you like to do that, Cooper?"

"Yes, I would!" he shouted, then, as though he remembered he was in a library and needed to use his indoor voice, he reduced his volume to a whisper. "Yes, I would."

"Then let's get these books checked out. Can you hand me your stack?" She reached over the shelf to gather Cooper's pile of books. A quick glance indicated last night's play had been a hit, as there was a reoccurring pirate and whimsical theme among the heap.

"Thank you, Scarlett." Miles followed her through the library toward the checkout window and came up beside her as she passed off the books to the librarian. "Thank you for doing this and for inviting us to join you at the play the other night and then again on your adventure today. It's nice to be included."

Before she could keep her mouth from verbalizing the thought flitting through her head, she said, "It's nice to have someone to include."

CHAPTER FIVE

*F*or a town that appeared to have no shortage of love to give, Miles was completely taken aback by the amount of homeless pets at the shelter. His bewilderment at the scene must have read like a novel across his face because Scarlett leaned close while they were receiving their volunteer instructions and whispered, "The Harmony Ridge Humane Society is a no-kill shelter, which means a lot of people from surrounding areas will surrender their animals here instead of their local ones."

That worked to settle his heart a little, as the thought of all the rejected pets originating from within Harmony Ridge itself didn't align with what he'd learned of the town thus far.

"Anyone have any questions?" A portly man with a handlebar mustache paced the floor in front of them, clipboard in hand. He had a cat draped across his shoulders like a shawl. Anywhere else it would have seemed an odd fashion statement, but here it worked. Plus, the man had explained that Seymour—the one-eyed, orange tabby with half a tail—was their longest resident at the shelter. Piggyback rides and extra attention were certainly in the cards for the senior cat.

"I'm going to start with the small dogs." Scarlett pulled a book at random from her tote and passed it to Miles. "Do you and Cooper want to go over with the large breeds?"

"I want to go with Scarlett," Cooper said. He already had her hand in his possessive grip.

"Only if it's okay with your dad."

"It's fine by me."

Miles slid the book under the crook of his arm and worked his way through the sterile building toward the kennels housing the larger animals. Each enclosure was outfitted with a dog bed, water and food dish, and some even had a couple of stuffed toys tossed in. But few dogs played with the toys, even fewer made eye contact as Miles shuffled past.

It was a depressing place and while reading might perk up the dejected animals temporarily, he knew it wasn't enough to fix their situations. It was a band-aid that would be ripped off the moment the volunteers left, a soothing balm that only disguised the under-lying pain but never quite took it away.

These animals didn't deserve to be in cold cinderblock cages; they deserved cozy places in front of fires, big, wide open yards to chase balls, and the loving consistency of a devoted owner to care for them.

If he let himself, Miles could easily slip into the same state of despair, but that wasn't what today was about.

He came to the end of the aisle, smack dab in front of a massive animal with slobber dripping from his mouth and sad, drooping eyes, almost cartoon-like in nature. He had to be some sort of horse-mix; Miles had never seen a dog so large.

"That's Waylon," the mustached volunteer offered, easing up behind them. He was a brave man to venture into the dog area with a cat strung around his neck, but it was almost as though the canines didn't even have the energy to care. "He's been with us for a few weeks."

"Great Dane?"

"Yep, mixed with something else, probably. Most of the dogs here are mutts, but those often make the best pets." The head volunteer clamped a hand down onto Miles' shoulder. "Good luck cheering this old boy up. I often say we should change his name to Eeyore. Poor guy is such a sad sack."

"Challenge accepted."

But Miles knew he'd have his work cut out for him. The life in this poor animal's eyes was all but extinguished. The way the dog surveyed Miles from behind the chain link as though sizing him up, then walking in one circle before plopping down in an exasperated huff, felt as close to an act of giving up as Miles had ever seen.

"Ah, come on, buddy." Miles lowered to the cold floor and cracked open the book. Of course, he hadn't taken the time to look at it prior to that moment. He probably should have. He doubted *Princess Patty Gets a Pony* would do anything to change Waylon's mood. The book was cute with glittery illustrations and sugary prose, but those weren't the ingredients for lifting Waylon's mood. He needed something more.

"Hey, Waylon?" Miles asked before he had the chance to feel foolish about talking to a dog. "You good with sitting tight for a moment while I go get something out of my car?"

The dog harrumphed, his jowls flapping with the expelled air.

"I'll take that as a yes."

Miles retraced his steps through the building and out to his truck in the lot. Maybe it was the fact that the dog's name was Waylon, maybe it was because music had always cheered Miles up—whatever the reason, he grabbed his guitar case from the truck bed and then reentered the shelter, finding Waylon in the same despondent heap.

"Got any requests?" he asked, slipping back down to the dog's level.

If a dog could roll his eyes, Waylon did just that.

"Fine. I've got a pretty decent repertoire I can cycle through. Let me know if you hear one you like."

The minutes in the following half hour blended into one other, just like the notes of one song rounded into the next. Miles thrummed through old set lists he still had committed to memory. He didn't sing along —other than occasionally harmonizing with Lana, that wasn't really his role, anyway. With each song, Waylon appeared less annoyed. He hadn't suddenly transformed into a happy-go-lucky pup, but his head lifted a little higher and there was a faint look of anticipation when one song would end and the beginning chords of another would lead in.

It felt good to play. How many days had it been since Miles had picked up a guitar, anyway? Five at the most. But that was the longest he'd gone without his fingers moving over the strings, and he'd missed it the way one missed a faraway loved one.

By the time the reading session was over, Miles was all in, strumming the guitar with unbridled enthusiasm. The standard poodle one cage over had started dancing along a few songs ago, a little prance and shuffling of paws that kept time with the beat. The chocolate lab behind them was in full-body mode, his zeal bursting right out of him in an energy consistent with the breed.

Even Waylon's mop of a tail swished back and forth on the concrete, though he hadn't moved from his sprawled position on the floor.

Still, Miles would take it as a win.

He wrapped up with the band's signature closing number, "Springtime Slowdown," and then placed the guitar into the case, confirming storytime was coming to an end with a look at his watch. Pushing up from the floor, Miles nearly knocked back over when Waylon bounded to his feet and wailed a cry worthy of a fire truck siren howl.

The dog sure had a set of pipes. Deafening ones. "It's okay, boy," Miles tried to soothe, but the piercing moan drowned out his calm voice. "Settle down, buddy."

"Are you guys okay?" Scarlett came racing around the corner, trying not to lose hold of Cooper's hand as she dragged him with her.

"Seems I've upset Waylon here."

Her gaze fell to the floor where the discarded book rested near the kennel. "The book was that bad, huh?"

"We actually didn't read it." He lifted his guitar case. "I opted for a little serenading instead, but I don't think he liked it."

"That, or he *loved* it and is upset it's over," Scarlett suggested. "Let's find out. Pull it out and play one more song."

Nothing about that request made Miles comfortable. So far, Scarlett hadn't pried too far into his past, and he felt good about keeping his life as a band member under wraps. But the embroidered band name across the guitar strap would be a dead giveaway, and he wasn't ready to answer the questions that would invite.

"You know, it's getting close to Cooper's naptime,"

he lied. Luckily, Cooper was too busy sticking his tongue out at the shaggy dog to his left that he didn't pipe up with the truth that he'd aged out of naptime months ago.

"I should probably head back to the Café too."

He was safe from her questioning for now, but he knew he could only buy so much time. At some point, she would wonder to the point of asking, and Miles just wasn't ready to answer.

The three walked back out of the shelter, Scarlett and Cooper hand in hand and Miles trailing a few feet behind.

Clearly, the kid had taken to Scarlett immediately, but that wasn't a hard thing to do. Miles already found himself wanting to get to know her better, and he found himself liking every new little thing he learned. Mostly, he appreciated her respect for the things he chose to keep private. She didn't force him to give up more than he wanted to about their detour, and that was the biggest breath of Harmony Ridge fresh air.

CHAPTER SIX

*S*carlett cut off the engine and sat a moment in the silence of the vehicle. She had every intention of heading back into the Café after her trip to the shelter, but the time counting down today's date on the calendar dwindled faster and faster with each passing minute, and she knew she couldn't put things off until tomorrow. By then, it would be too late.

The quiet in her car became a vacuum, the only sound her heart in her ears and the echo of her dad's voice in the memories that replayed like a reel in her mind. She worried someday she wouldn't be able to summon that voice so easily. That it would grow faint until it was altogether gone, like a balloon released into a cloudless sky, shrinking out of sight.

Through the windshield, bright and colorful blooms adorned her father's final resting place, right under the stately Heritage Oak in the center of the small-town cemetery. It had only been two years since his passing, but already there were fewer flowers left on this year's anniversary than the previous one. That was the way of grief, though. Eventually, people went through the stages and many even moved on from it.

Scarlett hadn't been able to move on. And she wasn't sure she even wanted to.

Reaching for the brown paper sack on the passenger seat, she nudged open her car door, lowering a foot onto the pavement.

She had stopped bringing flowers long ago. That hadn't been her relationship with her dad, something formal that required a bouquet of remembrance. She appreciated all the friends and family who thought to leave such beautiful tributes, but Scarlett and her dad shared something different.

After making her way through the quiet cemetery, she pulled two sandwiches from the bag and bent low next to his gravesite. "Brought your favorite." Setting the wrapped ham and Swiss onto the short grass, she crossed her legs to sit beside it.

The first time she'd done this—brought lunch for two to a graveyard—insecurity nearly kept her from seeing it through. It felt silly, in a way, to leave something so perishable. But she figured flowers were every bit as perishable. When it came down to it, everything in this life was.

The only things that didn't perish were faith, hope, and love. Her father had left her with all three, and Scarlett clung to those truths with an unwavering grasp.

"The Café's busier than ever." She munched into the sandwich and moved the back of her hand across her mouth. A sweet little chickadee trilled a tune from the branch above her. "Did you know the Henderson's still come in every Monday night for the prime rib special? Get all dressed up in their church best and everything. Say it's their standing date night. I've thought about pulling it from the menu a few times, but I just can't do that to them."

She could almost see the gleam in her father's eye, that crinkle that pushed them nearly closed each time he chuckled.

"When it comes down to it, I just can't make any changes, Dad." She settled the sandwich onto the open wrapper next to her and drew her knees up, letting her chin rest upon them. "I know you would want me to make the Café my own, but each time I think I'm ready to do that, it feels like I'm erasing a piece of you."

Fast-moving clouds above parted ways, releasing the once-hidden sunrays to cast over Scarlett's skin in a funnel of light that had her smiling at the sweet timing. It felt every bit as warm and protective as her father's big bear hugs. She closed her eyes, catching the tears before they could slip free.

"Mom's doing good," she carried on, if only to distract herself from the emotion welling within her. "She's become really involved in the Chamber of

Commerce. Helped put on the Chalk Walk and every-thing. You'd be so proud of her—how she's getting herself out there and keeping busy. She's been so strong." Flicking a piece of shredded lettuce off of the wrapper, Scarlett continued, "And Levi comes back from his honeymoon tomorrow. Can you believe, after all these years, he ended up with Chloe? I don't know how we didn't see that coming. They were right under our noses."

She knew her father would have grinned so widely at that. Chloe had been her brother's best friend throughout their entire childhoods. Their love was such a beautiful discovery and Scarlett felt blessed to have two of her favorite people find happiness in such an unexpected way.

"And before you ask, no, I'm not dating." She huffed through a little laugh. "I actually deleted that silly dating app you and mom kept telling me to download. I figure if I'm going to meet Mr. Right, it'll just happen. I don't need a computer program to initiate it."

Even though she'd been met with silence throughout the entire one-sided conversation, it was almost magnified now.

"You know I don't have time, Dad. The Café is all-consuming." Folding her half-eaten sandwich back into the paper, she sighed. "And I don't want you to think that's a burden for me. It truly isn't. Every day I wake up, I feel honored that I get to continue your legacy like this."

Of its own volition, her finger stretched out to trace the embossed grooves along the cold marble. *Jack Harmony, loving father, husband, and friend.* Her fingertip hung on the word *father* an extra moment, grateful she got to have him as hers, even if the spread between the dates under his name wasn't as long as she would have hoped.

"Thank you for the Café, Dad. I mean that. Thank you for letting me be the one to carry on with it. I know there were so many other people that you could have left it to that would've done a better job—or at least have been more qualified to do it. But for some reason, you chose me. I can't tell you how much that means. Your faith in me and your trust that I can do it. It's everything."

Her joints clicked as she pushed up from the ground and stretched to full height. In the distance, she could see Jimmy and Pamela Morgenstern's old powder blue Cadillac amble into the lot, a massive bouquet of yellow gerbera daisies obscuring Pamela's face from view. They were old bowling friends of her father's, and Scarlett knew right away they'd come to pay their respects.

Hurrying off with her things, Scarlett took a longer path back through the manicured graveyard toward her car. She knew she could stay and greet her dad's friends and there would be no problem with that—no sort of intrusion—but one thing about her father was that he made time for everyone. And as if reciprocating that, others continued to make time for him, even after he'd physically left this beautiful life.

Sure, some came to his grave to feel that closeness, but Scarlett knew just as many came to the Café to experience just a bit of that Jack Harmony nostalgia. And she would do everything in her power to make sure they always got it.

*a*t one point in time, Miles had a list of all the towns he'd visited, all the stages Timber Rose had walked onto and played upon. It was something his sister had encouraged, this tally of map dots. At first, it was like a game. A city scorecard to fill up. In reality, Miles rarely set foot outside of the arena or the blacktop where they parked the trailer. Sure, Lana would make each audience feel as though that particular venue was the only one that existed. She would make a real big deal of playing favorites, to the point of excess, always her MO.

"How are we doing tonight, Atlanta? You know we love performing for y'all. Hands down the best fans in this great big country of ours. But don't you go telling anyone. It's our little secret."

It didn't matter where they were. It was always the same. They would arrive, play their set list, and leave. Wash, rinse, repeat.

Miles didn't want that to be true of his time in Harmony Ridge. Originally, he'd planned to coast in and out, but something about the place tugged on his shirtsleeve, this urging to stay put and get to know the area. The people. The culture that was as small town as you could get.

Playing the tourist wasn't his thing, though. Local monuments and historical markers meant little when you didn't know the stories behind the people who put them there. He wanted full emersion, to become a part of the place. There was no better way to do that than to literally dig into the very ground the town rested upon.

"It says here you can even pick out one plant to bring home with you." With his finger hovering over the community garden's mobile website, Miles glanced at Cooper sitting next to him, spoon plunged into a bowl of colorful cereal, legs swinging beneath his chair without touching the floor.

"But we don't have a home, silly Daddy." The underbelly of the spoon pushed several O's below the surface of the milk. Cooper lifted the utensil, and they bobbed to the top again. He laughed, then crammed them down once more.

"We have a home." Miles tried to smooth out the tightness in his brow and in his voice. "Sure we do, buddy. It's you and me and whatever roof happens to be over our heads."

The boy shrugged and hoisted a mouthful of cereal to his lips. "Okay."

"Like right now, this Inn is our home." Miles could've let it drop, but the comment bombarded his focus and pinned him down. He couldn't get around it. "And sometimes the trailer we stayed in when Daddy would have concerts—that was our home too."

"Can I top you boys off?" Beth, the innkeeper, moved into the small dining room with a pitcher of fresh-squeezed orange juice in her grip and a hospitable smile on her face. She'd made sure they had all the comforts of home, from the hearty break-fast right down to the complimentary slippers in each room.

"I'd love some. Thank you, Beth." Pushing his empty glass closer for her to fill, Miles said, "I was just telling Cooper that home can be wherever you make it."

"Oh, absolutely." She brought the jug close to her hip and slanted her head. "I like to think this place becomes that to all the travelers who stay here. Might not be their permanent address, but it's home all the same. It's not home-forever, but at least it's home-for-now."

Whatever teaching moment he'd hoped to create had vanished, Cooper's attention shifted to the tabby cat perched on the windowsill behind them. The cat's long, striped tail swished below it like a hook dipped into water, swaying back and forth as Cooper tried to snag it with his hand, an eager fish ready to bite.

"Get on out of here, Bixby. Stop pestering our

guests." Beth shooed the feline from the window with her free hand, but the tabby didn't comply without first protesting with a displeased hiss. Drawing her chin down, Beth nodded toward the phone on the table. "You two going to the planting party today?"

"We were thinking about it."

"Oh, you definitely should. It's the sweetest little garden. I know Pearl could use the help too. It's entirely volunteer-run."

"Even the unfocused, four-year-old kind of help?" Miles' gaze reached his son.

"Of course. That's the best kind. There's no wrong way to plant something, you know. Given the right environment, a lot of love, and a little of God's help, anything can grow."

"How are those gloves fitting, buddy?"

Stretching his five fingers wide like a starfish, Cooper scrunched them into a fist, then popped them back open. "Good, I think."

A quick stop into Howie's Hardware supplied them with all they would need for a day in the dirt: a new pair of gloves each, two hand trowels, a small metal bucket to hold their things, and a bag of worms which Howie, the owner, insisted they would need. Since the worms were the gummy, edible kind, Miles could hardly refuse.

They walked up Harmony Ridge Row toward the

community garden at the end, and suddenly Cooper let out a shout. "That's Miss Scarlett's place! Let's go see her, Daddy."

"Oh, I don't know, Coop. She's working. She'll probably be busy. We don't want to bother her. Maybe another time."

It was too late for any sort of reasoning to reach Cooper's ears. The boy had picked up his pace and launched into an all-out skip that forced Miles to hustle to keep up. Even so, Cooper bounded into the entrance of the Campfire Café before Miles could grab the door.

"Is Miss Scarlett here?" Cooper asked the first person he saw, a young girl wearing a pin with the name *Katie* printed from a label maker. "I want to see Miss Scarlett."

"I'm sorry, kiddo. She's actually off today."

Shoulders lowering in a dramatic show of disappointment, the bucket in Cooper's grip met the floor with a noisy clatter. "Oh, man! That stinks."

"It's fine, buddy. We'll see her another time." Miles took his son's small shoulders into his grasp and offered a smile to Katie for the inconvenience. "Sorry to bother you."

"But I wanted to see her today!" Cooper wriggled free from his grip.

Katie looked the boy up and down. "You're not going down to the garden, are you?"

"I am." His brow remained bunched in discontent, his mouth puckered into an exaggerated frown.

Even the arms crisscrossed over his tiny chest showed his frustration.

"Hey, why don't you wait here one second?" She looked at Miles for confirmation, and he nodded.

Less than a minute later, Katie had returned with a small plastic baggie. Stooping to Cooper's height, she tucked the bag into his palm. "These are some extra sunflower seeds we've had from a dish our chef created a while back. I've been meaning to take them down to the garden to plant, but I haven't had any time. You think you could do that for me?"

"Yes, I can do that."

"Thank you, kiddo. That would be awesome." She popped back up. "Can I get you two anything else? A snack to take on the way? On the house."

"We've already eaten, but thank you." Miles swiveled Cooper back toward the door after thanking Katie once more and asking her to tell Scarlett they'd come by.

His head had obviously been elsewhere, otherwise Miles would have noticed the trail of discarded sunflower shells following them along their walk to the garden. By the time they arrived at the gate, there were only three remaining seeds in the baggie.

"Buddy, we were supposed to plant those for Katie. You weren't supposed to eat them all."

A guilty look splashed across the boy's face. "Oops." He covered his mouth, then looked down. "Maybe they will grow in my tummy!"

"That's not how it works. But hand me those last three so I can keep them safe."

Reluctantly, Cooper passed off the seeds, and Miles stuffed them into his pocket. "It said online to look for a lady named Pearl and that she'll give us all the instructions we need to get started."

"How do we know who Pearl is?"

"I suppose we can just look for her. She's got to be somewhere in these rows."

"Pearl!" Cooper megaphoned his mouth with his hands. "Oh, Pearl! Come out, come out, wherever you are!"

Like some game of hide-and-seek, an older woman with a silver bob emerged from the camouflage of lush greenery just a few paces away.

"Well, that's a superb greeting if I've ever heard one." Pinching her leather gloves from her fingers with her teeth, she clapped them together and jammed them into the back pocket of her overalls. "You must be Miles." Her calloused hand, weathered with age and gardening, slapped into Miles' firmly. "And I take it you're Cooper."

"Yes, ma'am." Cooper jutted out a hand and mimicked her assertive shake. "Nice to meet you."

"Well, it's certainly nice to meet you too, little fella. I'm so glad your daddy emailed about coming out today. I had a whole group of volunteers from the high school on the schedule, but evidently it's standardized test taking time and they had to move things around. So it'll just be the three of us playing in the dirt today."

"That's perfect because we only have three seeds." Cooper pointed with his index finger toward Pearl, then his dad, and then hooked it back toward himself. "One, two, three."

"You brought some seeds with you? Now that's certainly special."

"Katie down at the Café gave us some sunflower seeds to plant, but only a few made it in transit," Miles explained.

"I just planted my rows of sunflowers yesterday. And would you believe I came up exactly three seeds short?" Pearl took Cooper's hand into her own. "Come with me. I'll show you right where they will go."

Miles couldn't actually believe it—not so much Pearl's statement, but the sincerity of each person he'd come into contact with so far. Harmony Ridge was filled to the brim with caring people who sought to make life just a little bigger for his son. After so many years of adults trying to reduce Cooper to the point of invisibility, it was a gift Miles could scarcely wrap his head—and his heart—around.

CHAPTER EIGHT

*O*nce a month, Scarlett would allow herself a full day off of work. She'd spend that time catching up on the things needing attention around her small house. She'd finally comb through her stack of bills. Sometimes she'd get a haircut—tedious tasks that she put off until that empty day on the calendar.

But when she woke up that Thursday, none of those items felt as pressing as they had during the days leading up to it. She took her time getting ready, savoring a cup of medium roast coffee with a splash of honey on the couch while she watched a morning show in her pajamas. There was a stack of dishes in the sink, but she let them remain. They were good company for the dust bunnies that collected in the corners of her rooms and hallways.

Around ten, she showered and put on a little makeup, along with her favorite lavender V-neck tee and worn in boyfriend jeans. It was an unhurried beginning to her morning, the opposite of her bustling mornings at the Café.

By noon, the solitude began to wear on her. Sure, she could read a book or watch a movie in absolute quiet, but Scarlett was a people-person through and through. It wasn't a stretch to say she felt her light dim a little the further she got from her last social interaction.

Grabbing her phone, she shot off a text to Chloe. She adored her new sister-in-law—they had been friends for years before finally becoming relatives— and she knew some girl time would completely fill her cup.

Scarlett's modest townhome was just a short drive from Harmony Ridge Row. She swore the vehicle could make its way there all on its own and didn't need her at the helm to guide it, like her tires had created guiding grooves along the asphalt with the daily repetition. She pulled into an empty spot directly in front of Chloe's hand-lettering shop, Love Letters, and fed the meter a few coins before tugging on the storefront's door to open it wide.

"Good afternoon, my sweet friend!" Scarlett announced with flair, flinging her arms on either side, readied for the long-overdue embrace. "I have missed you so!"

On cue, Chloe leapt from her work desk and rushed across the shop. "Scarlett!" She pressed into

Scarlett's arms and the two women swung back and forth in a dance-like hug. "It's so good to be home."

"Sheesh! That honeymoon was a long one," Scarlett chided.

"It was. And I've got a gorgeous, golden tan to prove it."

Scarlett knew it wasn't about her, but it had been hard to go two weeks with no contact with her best friend or her brother. All three worked within a couple hundred feet of one another on Harmony Ridge Row, each running their own storefront. They were permanent fixtures in each other's days, and Scarlett felt their temporary absence deeply.

Maybe it was that absence that made Scarlett so clingy with Miles. Because she had been clingy, hadn't she? Her excitement over having someone to spend time with bordered on off-putting. Or so she figured. Miles hadn't given any indication that he'd viewed her multiple invitations as overzealous. Quite the opposite, in fact. He genuinely seemed grateful for them, that appreciation written all over his face and infused into his words. But then again, maybe he was just being nice. He seemed like a nice guy and that was the sort of thing nice guys did.

"You look well, Chloe." Scarlett admired her friend sweetly. "Marriage suits you."

"I've never been happier, Scarlett. Levi is my soul mate." Chloe nearly swooned.

"He's okay," Scarlett admitted with a shrug, only because she had to. As Levi's twin, it was her responsibility to give him a hard time, even though she agreed her brother and Chloe were the perfect match.

Chloe took Scarlett by the hand and guided her to sit on an empty rattan chair near her work desk. "So what's been going on around here while I've been gone? Give me all the Harmony Ridge latest."

There were things she could share, like the typo in the church bulletin that had turned the choir production into an evening of "fun and sinning," or the malfunctioning traffic light on Harmony Lane that sent the entire town into a tail spinning, tail light tizzy. But all she could think about was Miles.

How should she start? *'I met a guy'* didn't seem like an appropriate lead in, because they hadn't really met in that romantic kind of way. There wasn't anything going on between the two, and yet when she thought about him—the way he looked at her with his soulful, sapphire eyes, how he held the door open for her to walk through first, how he hung on her every word with devoted attention—she found herself filled to the brim with a swarm of fluttering butterflies, the kind that indicated feelings venturing outside the friendship realm.

"You haven't missed much, I promise," Scarlett said, finally. "Café's been busy. I hired a new girl, and it was a rough go at first, but I think she'll get the hang of things soon. They always do."

"Any interesting customers? That last story you told me about the one who stole an entire place setting of cutlery still makes me laugh every time I think about it. Not that the Café's utensils aren't lovely, but who wants used forks and spoons?"

This was Scarlett's opportunity to slide in the information about Miles. It wouldn't be strange to introduce him as a customer, especially since Chloe had implicitly asked about the very thing. Still, she worried the telling blush that crept across her cheeks would betray her, and no amount of denial would mask that.

"Customers have been woefully normal," she replied with a belabored sigh. "We could use a little more excitement around here, if you ask me."

"Oh, I don't know about that." Chloe lifted her shoulders to her earlobes. "After a week in Hawaii where there was an active volcano, a near shark attack, *and* a tidal wave warning, I'm all for woefully normal. At least, the sort of normal that Harmony Ridge has to offer."

For the next few moments, they scrolled through Chloe's images from the honeymoon on her phone. Levi and Chloe, all swimsuit clad and sun-kissed, looked the very picture of true love in each photograph. They raised fruity drinks together, lounged in the sun, and even drew a massive heart in the sand, with their initials carved into the very center.

Scarlett was thrilled for them. They deserved the love they had finally discovered in one another, so she couldn't make sense of the dull ache that came to her chest with each romantic image she viewed.

That wasn't ever anything she'd wanted for

herself. She was completely content with her single-hood—thrived in it, even. But a tiny niggling within made her wonder what it would be like to have someone to go through life with. Someone to share the ups and downs, hilltops and valleys, laughter and sorrow.

Her parents had had a beautiful, loving marriage, cut altogether short by a tragic traffic accident a couple of years back. She knew her mother wouldn't have changed anything had she known she would be a widow in her mid-fifties, but Scarlett witnessed the devastation of her mother's loss, and sometimes she felt like that was just as traumatic as if she'd witnessed the car crash firsthand. It all made her wonder if loving that deeply was worth the inevitable heartache that came when that love was cut short on this side of eternity.

She'd never gotten anywhere close to being in love. In high school, she'd have dates to the obligatory dances, but she never *dated*, per se. Rather, she rotated through seasonal sports, which left little extra-curricular time for much else. And that was the way she preferred it.

Even now, the Café was her reason for remaining single. Some may say she was married to her work, but that wasn't entirely a bad thing. She threw herself into it with all she had and vowed to make it a success. Would she even have anything leftover to give to someone if they came along?

"What aren't you telling me?" Chloe dipped her chin to lock in on Scarlett's contemplative gaze.

"I'm not not telling you anything."

"That's a double negative, and now I'm just confused." Her dear friend pursed her lips. "There's something you aren't saying, Scarlett."

And just like that, the bell chiming from above Chloe's door saved Scarlett, announcing another patron entering her little shop.

With all the reluctance that came with admitting defeat, Chloe stood to greet the shopper and Scarlett remained glued in place, staring blankly at the wall, wondering how she would worm her way out of this one. Chloe knew her well. She'd know if Scarlett was keeping something.

She would have stayed put had the voice that echoed back in greeting not been the very one Scarlett currently tried to put out of her head.

"Miles?" She rotated in her chair with a spin that nearly made her circle twice. She shot to her feet. Sure enough, Miles and Cooper filled up the entrance to the store, a delighted look of recognition splashing onto Miles' face.

"Scarlett. I didn't know you'd be here." He moved around Chloe and came up to…wait, was he going in for a hug? Scarlett jumped back and jutted out her hand for a shake instead.

Thrown off, Miles twitched his head, then grasped onto her hand.

"We just had some lunch at the Café and then thought we'd spend the afternoon strolling up and down the Row." He offered the explanation, but she really didn't need to be privy to his plans. "Plus, Cooper's looking for some artwork for our room at the Inn. Something to make it feel a bit more homey since we've decided to extend our stay a few days more."

"You're staying in Harmony Ridge?"

"I'm sorry." Chloe lifted her hands and flailed them about. "You two know each other?"

"Miles and Cooper came into the Café last week and then we saw the high school play of *Peter Pan* together."

"And we also read to doggies!"

Cooper suddenly reached for a framed piece of artwork and Miles intercepted just before the item toppled over. He righted the frame and secured his son's hand within his own.

Chloe flashed her friend a *'You've got some explaining to do'* look and then refocused her attention on making the sale.

"What specifically are you looking for? Something whimsical? Something inspiring?"

The store was filled with Chloe's hand-lettered creations, all beautiful works of art in their own right. Her talent with a pen was unparalleled and her ability to create brand new fonts by hand was a skill Scarlett would always admire. Without some guidance to narrow down, a shopper would want one of every print offered.

"Maybe a quote about home, if you have one," Miles suggested noncommittally. "Since we're trying to make our little space at the Inn feel more like one."

"I have lots of options for that. But if you don't see one you like, I can easily create a custom sign."

As she led him to the opposite end of the shop, Scarlett took the spare moment by herself to catch and hold her breath, something she usually didn't have to work hard at. But right now, all of her breaths were staccato, her heart rate punctuated with surprise. How did this man just show up right when she was thinking about him? In fairness, she found herself thinking about him a lot, so it wasn't a cosmic coincidence. Even so, the whole situation left her harried.

"What do you think about this?"

If she hadn't slipped so deeply into her thoughts, she wouldn't have leapt out of her skin like a crazy person. But she had been lost in la-la-land, so when Miles came up behind her and asked the question, both feet came off the ground.

"I'm sorry. I thought you heard me." He moved the print closer and asked again, "Do you think this is a good one?"

It was a sweet little drawing, with a simple water-colored house, white picket fence, and large apple tree in the front yard, complete with a tire swing dangling from a long branch. Above the illustration, in perfect block penmanship, it read: *Home is Wherever I'm with You.*

Though she had asked little about Miles' past, she

knew the father-son pair were on a grand adventure, and the saying was a beautiful fit.

"It's perfect."

"It's almost perfect." Chloe removed the piece from his grasp. "If you can come by here tomorrow morning, then it will be. I have a little something I want to add, but only if that's okay with you."

"Who am I to argue with the artist?" Miles' charm was undeniable, and even Chloe reddened at his compliment. "We'll be back tomorrow."

When he moved for his wallet, Chloe added, "You can pay when you pick it up."

"Alright. Sounds like a plan." He redirected Cooper away from a wall of glass-framed drawings and as the duo headed out the door, he called out, "I'll see you tomorrow."

Scarlett knew it was silly, but something in her hoped the comment was meant for her, even though he'd clearly said it to Chloe regarding the arranged pickup of the artwork.

What was going on with her?

"Are you okay?" As soon as the door swished shut behind Miles and Cooper, Chloe impaled her friend with a pointed look.

"I'm totally fine. Why?"

"Because you look star struck."

"Star struck?" Scarlett's chin pulled back. "Why would I be star struck?"

"Because *that* was Miles Callahan."

"I know his name. We've met, remember?"

Chloe looked at Scarlett like she'd fallen straight out of the tree in her painting. "You don't know who he is, do you?"

"Of course, I do. I told you, we went to *Peter Pan* and then to the shelter. We've hung out a couple times. We're friends," she said. "Sort of."

"Miles is from Timber Rose. Does that ring a bell?"

It sounded vaguely familiar, like when you can't quite place a face with the name. "Is that a town?"

"It's a band, Scarlett. I can't truly fault you because I know you only play instrumental music in the Café, but you really had no clue you were spending time with a guy from one of the hottest up-and-coming country groups?"

This was where she could either feel really stupid or just really naïve. And for some peculiar reason, she felt a healthy dose of both.

"I did not know he was part of a popular band," she said so matter-of-factly she sounded robotic.

"Gosh, he's really cute." With her gaze trailing out the window, Chloe half-sighed.

Scarlett walloped her on the shoulder. "You're a married woman!"

"I am, but I'm not blind."

Miles was obviously handsome and it would be crazy for Scarlett to think others wouldn't notice that. Suddenly, she felt all kinds of foolish for even allowing a romantic thought to pass through her brain. He was so out of her league, even more so now with his apparent rock star status and musical renown.

Why hadn't she realized this all sooner? And more importantly, why hadn't he mentioned anything to her?

CHAPTER NINE

*I*t was the third time that day that he'd sent the call straight to voicemail. He wasn't sure how much longer he'd be able to do that before Lana tried to contact him in an alternate form. Once, when he hadn't returned her drunken midnight dial immediately, she even took to Twitter to track him down.

"If someone can get ahold of Miles Callahan for me, please tell him his bandmate desperately needs him."

That, of course, made the internet devolve into couple conspiracy chaos. There had been romantic rumors swirling around them for years, none of which Miles ever added any fodder to. Sure, they'd been together in the past, and though he would never in his life say Cooper was a mistake, wasting emotion on a woman devoid of real human connection wasn't a wise thing to do.

He'd been prepared for this. He knew his swift departure would be the starting point in her quest for answers. But he knew he didn't owe her any. Of that, he was certain.

After a long, thorough talk with his agent, Miles had been given the green light to exit the band. They'd recorded their first album, fulfilled their promised tour dates, and finished out their contract. Of course, anyone would assume they would immediately head back into the studio to capitalize on their rising success. It would be foolish not to.

But the interest just wasn't there for Miles. It had been a wild ride, and he couldn't say the experience was altogether unenjoyable. That would be a lie. There was something about playing before sold-out crowds. A reciprocal energy that only a musician could truly understand. At one point in his life, he absolutely loved it. That rush. That high. The way sharing music with others was almost a holy experience.

Becoming a dad had changed things.

He didn't suddenly become a dud who didn't know how to let loose or have fun. But his priorities realigned and he would never let them jumble into a different order ever again.

Cooper was his everything. His number one.

And right now, that everything was curled in a ball on their queen-sized bed, teddy bear sandwiched under his arm, thumb thrust into his mouth.

Every once in a while, when Cooper was deep in

slumber, he'd suck his thumb like that. It made him look like the sweet baby he once was, the chubby little infant with rolls upon rolls and a contagious giggle that could make a grown man burst into hysterics. He had always been such an easygoing baby, not that Miles had anything to compare him to. But it was a gift to have a little one that seldom cried; Miles knew the worth of that.

From day one, it had been just the two of them. Miles sometimes wondered if that would always be the case. In truth, he tried to keep his mind from wandering in that direction. They were the perfect team, just Cooper and Miles. There seemed little need for anyone else.

But the way Scarlett had so easily engaged with Cooper was undeniable. How she held his hand and treated him like the valued person he was. She didn't discount his feelings or ideas just because he was a young child. That was remarkable. *She* was remarkable.

For the first time in a long while, Miles felt something. Some stirring in his heart, like it was tapping from within him, trying to get his attention. Trying to let him know it was still in there. What was he to do with that?

When Lana's name scrolled across Miles' phone screen for the fourth time that evening, he shut the device off completely. It felt like a safe enough thing to do. They'd already had their nightly phone time with his sister, and he wasn't expecting any other calls.

Securing the quilt up to Cooper's shoulders, Miles grabbed the monitor from the nightstand and quietly exited their room. With the monitor tucked into his belt loop, he walked down the hall toward the spiral staircase that led down to the main level.

Harmony Ridge had proven to be a safe community. He was sure Cooper would be fine slumbering in their locked room while Miles enjoyed a cold drink on the porch of the Inn, but the baby monitor gave him an extra layer of confidence that if his son should need him, he would be just a few paces away.

Still, even though there was only one flight of stairs between them, Miles felt that missing piece, that Cooper-shaped hole. Other than Maddie, no one ever watched his son. There wasn't much need for a sitter, really, apart from when Miles played at concert venues where children were prohibited. As an infant, Cooper even tagged along with Miles to the recording studio. He'd line his guitar case with receiving blankets and tuck Cooper right into it, letting the baby slumber in the empty outline of his stringed instrument.

Initially, he thought all the time Lana spent around her young son would've awoken some maternal instinct within her. Maybe that's what Miles was trying to do. Love by forced proximity. He wasn't sure. But the truth was, he enjoyed having his son around. He assumed Lana would too.

Still, Miles knew a time would come when his life would diverge from his son's. Miles prayed it wouldn't come until Cooper was well into his teens, but he didn't delude himself. Cooper was his own person. So was Miles, even though some days he really didn't feel like it.

He made his way into the kitchen, helping himself to one of the complementary drinks in the fridge that Beth had showed him upon arrival. The Adirondack rockers had been calling his name all week, and the wraparound porch with its perfect view of Harmony Lane was something out of a storybook he wanted to slip into the pages of.

Finding the bottle opener in a basket of communal items on the island in the kitchen, Miles popped the top off of a cream soda. The slow hiss of carbonation harkened back to childhood memories of when his sister would drive to the gas station after school, a handful of crisp ones for Miles to buy whatever he wished. That was occasionally a pile of candy, but more often than not, an amber bottle of cream soda. He knew Maddie's retail job at the local shopping mall didn't provide her with much extra spending cash, but she always shared whatever she had with her younger brother. Her love language was generosity, and she routinely blessed Miles with it.

As he toed open the screen door tonight and stepped out onto the porch, reveling in the sweet memory like a hug, he wished Maddie could join him for an evening drink. He'd missed her camaraderie and closeness more than he'd realized.

But even if Maddie had been in Harmony Ridge,

she wouldn't have been able to join him on this particular porch. The extra seat was already taken.

"Eugene," Miles greeted, surprised to see the old man moving the rocker back and forth with a push from his leather loafer. "I didn't realize you were staying here too."

Finding the empty chair next to him, Miles settled in.

"Oh, I'm not staying here." Eugene shakily lifted his own bottle—something a little stronger than cream soda—to clink against Miles'. "Beth lets me hang out on this old porch whenever I like." He drew in a long swallow of his drink and thrust a fist to his chest when a small burp chased it. "I used to have a porch just like this one, and a whole big, beautiful house to go with it."

Miles rocked his chair, matching the slow, creaky speed of the one next to him. "That so?"

"Yep. Got to be too much for me to care for on my own once my wife, Doris, passed. Too much house for just one person, you know? Even though I was always there, it just felt empty."

Miles tipped his chin in a nod.

"Moved into assisted living some five or so years ago." Eugene paused to wave at a young mom rolling a stroller down the path in front of the Inn. "How sad does that sound? To need assistance living? But I guess we all need a little help every now and again." He scrunched his frail shoulders up to his ears. "I have my own little apartment with a small balcony where I keep a few fake plants, just because I know I'd kill the real ones. But I still like the greenery, and I sure do miss my porch. So I come here a few times a week, just to relax and get my neighborly fix. It's good for my soul. Sometimes I pretend I own the whole place, just for kicks. Pretend that all the guests inside are my family members. I'm not crazy, but I've got a big imagination."

"I think that's really great, Eugene. We all need community."

"Don't get me wrong. There are a lot of people at the place I live," he said. "They're just all really old."

Miles had a hard time not chuckling at the irony of it all.

"You settling in to Harmony Ridge okay?" When an old sedan leisurely rumbled by, Eugene offered another wave. The driver tooted the horn in response and the old man's entire face lit up with delight.

"The goal isn't really to settle. But yes, we're enjoying ourselves."

"You also enjoying Scarlett Harmony?"

Miles choked on his soda, the fizzy burn bubbling up his throat. "Scarlett?"

"Oh, you two aren't dating?"

"No." Miles shook his head. "We're not dating."

"I just assumed two good-looking, single people would want to date one another. Silly me."

"It's not silly," Miles said. "Just surprising."

"You do think she's beautiful, don't you?" Eugene waved again and this time his greeting went unacknowledged by the runner sprinting by with earbuds shoved deeply into his ears. He frowned.

Miles didn't know how to answer. "Of course, she's beautiful."

"But not your type?"

That was the thing. Miles didn't know if he even had a type, but everything about Scarlett was something he'd add to a list had he ever made one. She was selfless, engaging. Motivated in her work and career. Her carefree spirit was contagious. All of those unwritten boxes were checked off one by one.

But dating wasn't in the cards. Miles came to Harmony Ridge on his route to stability and nothing was stable about the dating scene, he knew that much.

"I'm not really in the market to date."

"Things complicated with the boy's mom?" Maybe it was his age that made Miles offer Eugene a little grace, but he wasn't actually put off by the probing question.

"She's not in the picture." He pushed his chair all the way back before letting it fall forward again.

"That's not something you often hear of—a mom that's uninvolved."

Oh, Lana was more than just uninvolved. She was completely absent.

"We're an anomaly. What can I say?"

Eugene's hand came down onto Miles' knee and cupped it with a clap. "You're doing right by him. That boy doesn't seem to want for anything; you can see it."

"Sometimes I wish I could give him more than just me. A family, you know? He needs that."

A twinkle came to Eugene's eye, and he took another full swig from his bottle before he said, "I own this place, remember?" He winked and added, "You're *my* family now."

CHAPTER TEN

*I*t was kismet that the soup of the day was chicken noodle. Scarlett ladled out a double portion into a large Styrofoam bowl with a lid, and placed it into a paper bag, along with several slices of a fresh baguette from her brother's bakery.

Cooper might not feel up to eating it right away, but she also tossed in an iced sugar cookie in the shape of a robot for a sweet treat.

When she'd gotten a text from Miles earlier that morning, her heart had initially done a full-on cartwheel when his name blipped on her screen, only to plummet and crash when she took the time to read his words.

Poor Cooper was sick with a fever and a nose that ran like a faucet. Miles had requested that Scarlett relay the information to Chloe and ask forgiveness for missing their appointment to pick up the artwork from her store.

Scarlett did all of that, but knew feeling under the weather in a place that wasn't familiar was downright miserable. And while the Inn was a great place to stay and had many of the comforts of home, she knew the soup Beth had to offer likely came from a can. That just wouldn't do.

She decided not to text Miles on her way, mostly because she didn't want him to politely decline, which she figured he would. If she'd learned anything about the man, it was that he didn't like to put others out.

"Hi, Beth." Scarlett entered the foyer and caught sight of the innkeeper dusting a gilded frame on the wall.

She'd always loved this Inn and the historical charm it boasted. Even though she was local, Scarlett would rent a room for the night on occasion, just to mix things up with her routine. If that wasn't a testament to her love for this town—that she preferred to vacation within her very zip code—then she didn't know what was.

"Would you mind letting Miles know I'm here? Just stopping by with a little something." Scarlett hoisted the bag up to eye level.

"Oh, I can smell it already. Makes my mouth water." Beth rested the duster on the check-in desk. "I'll call right up to him and have him come down to get it."

"Thank you. Appreciate it."

Scarlett moved to the drawing room and sat in the high-back chair angled a few feet off the fireplace.

Though it wasn't lit, the hearth added a warmth to the otherwise formal space. It wasn't hard for Scarlett to envision families enjoying this cozy spot throughout the generations.

The Inn had belonged to her great-great-great-grandfather before it ever housed travelers and tourists. Sometimes she wondered why it hadn't been passed down through their own family tree, but to her credit, it was too much house for her to maintain on her own. Historic homes came with their own unique challenges, often in the form of faulty foundations, infestations of termites, or peeling paint. The Inn on Harmony Lane sure had her fair share over the years, and it had been a wonder the old structure was even still standing.

But Scarlett was grateful for Beth and her devotion to this place. The woman had been running it for the last dozen years and she made every traveler who passed through Harmony Ridge feel as welcome as a long-time resident. And she proved you didn't need to be related to one of the town's founders to appreciate the rich history of the community and have a passion for keeping it preserved.

Scarlett heard footfalls only moments later, but when Miles rounded the bannister and came into the room, she still had to work to conceal her shock. He was entirely unkempt, with patches of hair jutting out in multiple directions and purple bags slung under bloodshot eyes.

"Hey." She stood and stretched her arm out to

hand off the bag. "I brought you and Cooper a little something for lunch. Chicken noodle. I hope you don't mind."

He raked a hand through his disheveled hair first and then reached for the bag, seemingly a little thrown off at the gesture. "Oh. Wow. You didn't need to do all of that. I hope you didn't think that I was hinting by my text."

"No, no. Not at all. Our soup of the day just so happened to be the world's greatest cure for the sniffles. It felt a little selfish hoarding it all at the Café."

His tired eyes lifted in a smile of utter thankfulness. "That was very thoughtful of you, Scarlett. I'm sure Cooper will love it. When he wakes up, that is."

"Oh, he's sleeping? That's good. The best thing he can do."

"It is, especially since we were up all night."

She'd already put that together from Miles' appearance. "Is there anything else I can do while I'm here? Run some errands for you? Swing by the grocery store?"

He paused like he was about to say something, but then nothing followed.

"Well." She clapped her hands to her thighs. "I guess I'll be—"

"Would you like to stay for a bit?"

"Oh." She hadn't been expecting that. "Yes. Sure, I would."

"I'm not going to invite you up because I think our room is littered with dozens of crumpled tissues, but I was going to go for a stroll out back in the gardens, if you'd like to join me. I need some fresh air."

"I would love to." It surprised her how much she wanted to join him, in fact.

They stopped through the kitchen on their way to the back of the house, and Miles placed the soup in the cupboard Beth had reserved for him during their stay. It would keep in there just fine until they returned from their walk and Miles would be able to take it up to Cooper.

Scarlett trailed closely, noting the monitor that dangled from his belt loop. The volume dial was turned down low, but she could still make out the raspy breathing of sweet Cooper as he caught up on some much needed rest.

Miles was a good father, full of unconditional love for his son. Something about that made Scarlett's own heart ache with tenderness. She'd never been attracted to a man with a child before, as she knew that brought with it an entirely new bag of complexity. But she wondered if the fact that Miles was a father actually had something to do with her growing feelings for him. It was as though she'd experienced another layer of him—his compassion, his nurturing spirit. She saw the way he loved effortlessly, and it inspired her.

"You been back here before?" he asked once they were out of the old house and into the streams of late-May sunshine.

There was a low picket-fence gate a few yards up that led into the gardens in the rear of the property. He opened it once they made their way over. Instantly, the scent of fresh lavender hit Scarlett's senses, and the bees and monarchs that bounced from flower to flower ushered in all the springtime feels.

"I helped plant it, actually." For some strange reason, she felt a little silly sharing that information. "Beth had a big volunteer day a few years back after a hundred-year flood wiped out the original crop. My particular section was right over here." She walked him through the decomposed granite pathways toward the manicured rows of lavender, all delicate purple stalks that swayed in a soft breeze. "Lavender grows really well in this climate, so I can't take credit for how beautifully the plants have thrived over the years. But I dug the holes and dropped the original plants into them, so that might count for something."

"I think you can take credit." Miles looked at her thoughtfully, as though sizing her up with sincere gratitude. "These are beautiful, Scarlett."

"Lavender is an incredible flower. Beth makes oil from these particular plants. There are a few varieties that we use in the Café in our lemonades and espresso drinks." She reached out with the tip of her finger and touched the plant closest to her. "And it's great for creating calm. I have several sachets I keep in my bedroom and I swear they help me sleep when my mind won't shut off."

There was an old iron bench nearby under an

arbor of pink rambling rose blooms, and she lowered to sit, hoping Miles would take the open seat next to her. He did, and their legs touched. She tried not to withdraw, but the close proximity made her heart gallop like a racehorse let out of the starting gate.

"I could use a little help with that," he admitted. "Getting my mind to shut off."

"Overactive imagination?"

"No, just a big over thinker."

She could tell something plagued him by the way he gazed off in the distance without focusing on anything in particular, his brow drawn low over pensive blue eyes.

"Anything you care to talk about?"

His hand came to rest on his leg, the one right next to hers, and she suddenly felt like a teenager in a movie theater, arm perched on the rest, hoping to have her hand held for the first time. But she folded hers together in her lap instead and prayed she hadn't said too much.

"I don't want to bother you with my troubles." He shook his head.

"It wouldn't be a bother."

He turned a little and looked at her straight on. Then, before allowing himself to change his mind, he said, "Before coming here, I was in a band."

"Timber Rose," she spoke for him. She'd gotten over her displeasure about not knowing from the start. It wasn't about her. Miles was entitled to keep whatever areas of his life private that he wanted. She'd come to respect that.

"Yeah, that's the one. But I left."

"Left the band completely?"

Miles nodded solemnly. "It's really complicated."

"I hear band relationships can be." She knew nothing about band life, but she wanted to offer a sympathetic ear and it felt like the right thing to say in the moment.

"One of my band members is Cooper's mom."

Scarlett's spine went ramrod straight. "Oh," she murmured. "I didn't realize she was in the picture."

"She's not. That's the whole thing. Lana has never even acknowledged that Cooper is hers."

"Seems a little hard to deny since I'm assuming she was there for the birth." Scarlett let the words fly without a filter. "I'm sorry. It's not my place to say that."

"No, you're exactly right. But she signed over her parental rights to me from the beginning, complete with a whole court case and everything. I've had full custody of Cooper ever since."

"I'm so sorry, Miles. That must be really difficult."

"Yes, and no." He took a large breath that elevated his shoulders. "It's not as though I want her to be involved. She wouldn't be a good mother. She's too selfish for that. I just feel like Cooper deserves someone to love him and nurture him."

"He already has that," Scarlett affirmed. "He has you."

"Sure, but sometimes I feel like I'm not enough."

"You know? I don't think parenting is a one-size-fits-all sort of thing. And I don't think you need to have the love of two parents to feel complete. Love expands and fills up the empty spots."

"I like that. I just hate to think that he even has an empty spot to begin with."

Miles held her gaze for so long she became aware of her staggered breathing. When he reached down and pulled her hand from her lap to thread her fingers with his, Scarlett's stomach quivered with a tremble of both nerves and longing.

He locked eyes again. "Is this okay?"

"Yes." Her grip tightened around his. "It is."

"Thank you."

"For holding your hand?"

He chuckled. "I mean, sure. Thank you for letting me hold your hand, but what I really meant was thank you for reassuring me that I'm doing right by Cooper." His thumb brushed along the smooth skin on the back of her hand and she couldn't ignore the shivers that skittered up her spine with each swipe of his skin on hers. "And for being you. Doing things to make us feel included here like inviting us along on your adventures and bringing us soup. I like you, Scarlett. I hope it's okay for me to say that."

"I like you too, Miles." She'd never said the words to anyone before, and yet they didn't feel scary when someone like Miles was the one on the receiving end.

"Do you think we'd be able to do this again?"

"Sit in the garden?"

"Sure." He laughed again softly. "Or go on a date?"

"Oh." She hadn't meant to sound surprised.

"We don't have to——"

"I would love that, Miles."

He grinned and shook his head, likely thinking better of his sudden proposition. "I'm not sure about the logistics of that. Four-year-olds don't make great date companions and I don't really have anything in the way of childcare."

"We'll figure it out," she assured. "I really don't mind if Cooper tags along. I like his company."

"I do too, but I also want to feel like a man for one night, not just a father. And that involves taking you on a proper date where I pay and we can have adult conversation and I don't have to worry about Cooper breaking anything or spitting out the food he doesn't like at the dinner table."

She couldn't keep the smile from her lips, easily envisioning the very thing. "I think I have the perfect option. When are you free?"

CHAPTER ELEVEN

"*Y*ou got everything you need, Coop?" Miles handed Cooper the space shuttle backpack Aunt Maddie had given him last Christmas. The boy shouldered into it. "Water bottle?"

"Check." Cooper thrust a finger in the air, ticking items off an imaginary list.

"Orson?"

"Check."

"Giant sword to fight off any smelly dragons or ugly ogres you might come across during your day's adventures?"

"Silly, Daddy. I don't have a sword."

"Oh," Miles played along. "My mistake."

It was the second time that week that he had left Cooper with Scarlett's brother, Levi, at the bakery. While everyone seemed more than okay with the setup, guilt still weighed heavily on Miles' chest.

Scarlett had painted her brother out to be the picture-perfect babysitter, and he certainly lived up to that glowing praise. Prior to opening his bakery, Levi had been a firefighter, so he was certified in all the things that mattered when it came to safety. Plus, as a newlywed, it was good for him to spend time with kids —a sort of "parental preparedness crash course" as Scarlett had coined it.

Miles trusted Scarlett, so he took her at her word, and Levi proved to be cut from the same capable cloth as his sister. That was a comfort. Leaving Cooper in his care that first time—even though it was just under an hour—wasn't as scary as Miles anticipated it might be.

Plus, Cooper had spent that entire evening talking animatedly about Levi and their baking adventures. How they rolled out the dough and made "millions of cookies" with cutters and shapes. The icing was Cooper's favorite. Miles wondered if the boy had possibly bathed in a vat of the sugary stuff before he was returned into Miles' care. It was crusted behind his ear, matted in his hair, and stuck to his clothes like an edible glue.

Miles wasn't the sort of parent to worry about sugar rushes or toothaches, so none of that bothered him. He knew full-well his sister spoiled Cooper relentlessly. But that's what aunts and uncles were for. Not that Levi was an uncle, but the label felt the same.

Cooper tugged on his dad's pant leg twice. "Can we *please* go in now?"

Stuttering out of his thoughts, Miles nodded, then crossed the sidewalk to grab the door handle to Perfect Harmony Bakery. Instantly, the warm, buttery scent of croissants cocooned them like a freshly baked hug. It was a carbohydrate heaven and Miles was tempted to order one of every item within the pastry case, but he wanted to save his appetite. He had big plans for his date with Scarlett.

"Cooper Trooper!" Levi bounded from the back kitchen, shouting gleefully as he skirted the counter to scoop the boy into a hug that lifted his small feet from the ground. "There's my baking buddy!"

Maddie had often called Cooper by the same affectionate nickname and something about the coincidence pulled at Miles' heartstrings.

Levi's excitement wasn't for show. His face genuinely reflected his gusto over Cooper's arrival. That made leaving again today even easier, and Miles freed himself of the guilt he'd unknowingly stored up.

"Look what I got for you, dude." With Cooper on his hip, Levi moved back near the cash register and pulled a piece of baby blue fabric from a shelf below, then slung it around the boy's neck. "Your very own apron!"

"No way!" Cooper tugged at the hem. "What does it say?"

Levi drug his index finger under the lettering across the chest as he read aloud, "*Perfect Harmony Bakery*. Property of Cooper Callahan." Looking over at Miles, Levi apologized, "Sorry I sent him home looking like he was caught in a confectionary hurricane last time. We'll try to be a little less messy today."

"Where's the fun in that?" Miles lifted a brown lunch sack and deposited it onto the counter. "I packed some snacks for later. Fed him a light dinner, but he might get hungry again before I'm back to pick him up. I think the kid has a hollow leg."

"I've got the food department completely covered," Levi assured. "You like pigs in a blanket, Cooper Trooper?"

The child burst into giggles. "Pigs in a blanket," he repeated, likely envisioning the farm animals wrapped up tightly in quilts. "That's silly."

"Oh, buddy, it's delicious. I've got the dough rolled out in the back already. All we have to do is add the hot dogs."

"I thought you said pigs!" Cooper squealed.

"Yeah, I don't actually know why they call them pigs. Should be dogs in a blanket. Puppies in a pastry?"

All three laughed at that and after confirming the time he would return to pick up Cooper—followed by Levi reiterating that they would be just fine for as long as Miles cared to stay out—Miles left the bakery to walk up the Row toward the Café.

It was great to see Cooper so settled. Miles knew there were kids who would dissolve into a puddle of tears each time a parent left. Separation anxiety was no joke. But Cooper was so resilient, so easily adaptable. The kid was amazing. Even when he'd been sick earlier that week, he didn't complain, just took the extra downtime to enjoy calmer activities like coloring and cuddling versus playing at the park or zooming around on his scooter.

But it was good to see Cooper operating at one-hundred percent again. A sick child was always a worry, even when it was just a common cold.

"Hi, Miles," Timmy greeted when Miles entered the Café, a stack of menus in hand. "Scarlett's in the back. I'll let her know you're here."

"Great. Thanks, man." Scanning the restaurant, Miles noted just how busy it was, patrons filling nearly every empty table. Even the barstools at the long counter were all spoken for, and usually there were a few to spare.

Making himself comfortable near the hostess podium, he crossed his arms and waited for Scarlett to emerge. For a moment, he wondered if she might need to cancel. With the growing crowd of restaurant goers, it was likely they would require all hands on deck. Was it selfish to take her away when she was obviously quite needed?

"Miles!" Scarlett finally bounded from the kitchen, lifting the counter hatch as she passed through. "Sorry to keep you waiting. I had to make sure everyone was on the same page before I bowed out for the night. But I'm good to go now."

"I haven't been waiting long. You sure you still want to go out? It looks like you guys are really busy."

"We are, but I've got a great staff and they've got

things under control. Plus, I've been looking forward to this all day. It's what helped me hobble to the finish line of the lunch rush earlier." She pulled on a jean jacket from the coatrack by the door and slid her purse strap up her arm and onto her shoulder. "You ready to get going?"

"I sure am."

He looked at her a moment, noting the darker shade of her lips, covered in a deep pink gloss. Her eyes had a shimmery powder on their lids, and it made them shine even more brightly than usual. And if he wasn't mistaken, she'd even taken the time to add a few loose curls to her long blonde strands. She was breathtakingly beautiful and the thought that she might've done all of this for her evening with Miles made him smile appreciatively.

"I'm parked just a little way up the road. I'm happy to get the truck and drive back to pick you up if you don't feel like walking."

"No, I'm good with walking." She took his hand in hers.

The act was bold and altogether delightful. Miles found himself adopting an even slower pace, just to prolong the moment and savor the feel of her hand in his.

"I was going to book us a dinner out, but then I realized the town really only has two restaurants: yours, and then another called Interlude, which felt a little fancy for a first date."

"Oh, that place is totally pretentious. Don't get me

wrong. It's really nice, if you like ordering food you can't pronounce and then paying an arm and a leg for said unpronounceable food."

"That's kind of the vibe I got from the website, so I came up with something a little different."

Once at the truck, Miles rounded it to open the passenger door for Scarlett. He waited until she was situated in her seat with the belt across her lap before closing the door and joining her around the other side.

"I'm up for different. Honestly, I'm just looking forward to any kind of conversation that doesn't involve a list of the day's specials or directions to the restroom."

"Noted. I'll be sure to avoid those two topics."

He steered the truck from the curb and traveled down the road. Over the minutes, they fell into effortless conversation. Scarlett shared more about her family and even surprised Miles when she brought up her father's accident, which had happened much more recently than Miles had thought. The grief was shaky in her voice and she spoke of her relationship with her father with such genuine fondness that Miles felt like he knew the man by the end of the conversation. Or at least, it made him wish he'd had the chance to know him.

Miles could see how Scarlett had inherited her father's love for people—and his love for feeding people. The Campfire Café had been his true calling in life, his way to intentionally build relationships and commune with the people he loved. It was as though the restaurant was his church, the place where her father carried out God's purpose for him.

She never asked where they were going while they drove, and the trust that indicated made Miles' heart swell with pride. Several moments later, when he angled into the tree-covered park in the neighborhood right next to the Inn, her face bloomed with recognition.

"You brought me to the farmers' market?" Her tone was thick with emotion. "Miles, this is perfect!"

"I was thinking we could go around to the different booths and pull together a meal for tonight and enjoy it here. There's a big grassy area on the east side of the park that I noticed when Cooper and I visited last week. I've got a picnic basket in the back of the truck, along with a blanket. It's a little bit of a makeshift dinner out, but I hope it'll do."

"It'll more than do. I love it." She unbuckled her seatbelt and paused a breath, taking him in. "You couldn't know this, but coming to this very market is one of my favorite activities. I just never get to attend because I'm always at the Café on Thursday nights."

"Then I'm glad I could steal you away for just one evening and make it happen."

"I'm hoping you'll steal me away for more than one," she said, and then jumped down from the truck before Miles could register the bold flirtation in her statement.

They collected the wicker basket and fell into step

with the other neighbors and market attendees, moseying up and down the rows of pop-up tents and food trailers.

Scarlett stopped at each booth. She asked every vendor about their product and her interest wasn't false. She was genuinely awed by the whole thing. Even the way she would pick up a piece of fruit and roll it in her hand, admiring its freshness and perfect shape, was like a kid in the biggest of candy stores.

Miles was happy to carry the basket, which they filled to the brim within mere minutes of their arrival. Scarlett had tossed in honey and rich creamy cheeses, jams and locally made salamis. They purchased a crusty baguette, and she admitted she felt a bit like she was cheating, what with her brother owning a bakery and all. They agreed that even if it was the best loaf of bread they'd ever tasted, they would never confess that to Levi.

Honestly, Miles could have spent the entire evening strolling the venue with Scarlett. Even though she was a local, her zeal for the experience was endearing. He was thankful—honored, even—he got to share it with her.

He was thankful for *any* moment he got to spend with Scarlett.

When the basket threatened to burst open at the bottom, they agreed they likely had enough ingredients to make a hefty meal. It just so happened that there was a winery pop-up offering tastings and bottles for purchase, so they grabbed a bottle of the red and snagged two paper cups from a nearby drinking station.

"Does over there look good to you?" Miles dipped his head toward a slopping green several yards up with massive weeping willows curtaining perfectly placed picnic tables and benches.

"That looks great," she agreed. They set out toward a patch of open grass.

Miles tried not to feel insecure, but he knew he was just the visitor here, and something about that made him feel a little silly about taking charge. In reality, Scarlett should be the one calling the shots for their evening. She certainly knew more about Harmony Ridge than he ever could. But Miles had wanted to take her out—treat her to a special time where she didn't have to think about or plan anything. Scarlett appeared more than happy to oblige, so Miles continued to take the lead. And he would for as long as she let him.

He lowered the basket onto the grass first, then pulled the folded quilt from under his arm and flapped it open before letting it slowly settle to the ground like an autumn leaf released from a branch. He had told Beth about his plans earlier in the day and she'd instantly rushed to the linen closet to retrieve a worn but suitable picnic blanket, saying it was absolutely necessary for the evening he had envisioned.

She had been right. It was a nicely put together quilt, but a little on the small side, which was absolutely fine by him. That would just mean they would have to sit closer together. Miles wondered if maybe that had been the purpose of the borrowed quilt all along.

The breath of sheer delight Scarlett released once she settled onto the picnic blanket was all the affirmation Miles needed. This had been his hope: to offer Scarlett an evening to let go and completely relax. It appeared she was able to accomplish just that.

Over the next hour, they snacked on bunches of sweet grapes, ate olives with pits that they made a game of spitting clear across the lawn, and wound things down with a glass of wine in their paper cups, along with a brick of dark chocolate which they split evenly.

Come sundown, vendors began to pack up their wares and even the jazz band wrapped up their final song, the notes trailing off and into the air like wisps of a dandelion wish. The flood lights that had kept the event going into dusk flickered off one by one. The only thing left to illuminate the park was the waning sun as it slowly slipped into the horizon, but not before giving off the brightest pink and orange hued sunset Miles had ever witnessed.

The evening had the makings of a perfect one, with the exception of one last thing.

Miles looked over at Scarlett leaning back on her elbows at the edge of the quilt, face inclined skyward. She had her eyes fixed ahead, as though replaying the beauty of the setting sun in her mind based on the wistful smile still clinging to her lips. Her profile was captivating, and he found himself wanting to sweep away the soft strands of hair that swirled over her face as the breeze picked up around them.

"This is just what I need," she said, her voice full of contentment. She sat upright and leaned forward. "*You* are just what I need."

Miles moved closer. Scarlett tilted her head to face him. Their eyes met, and he gently lifted his hand to touch her chin. He tried not to second guess himself when he let his mouth find hers. Her lips eagerly pressed back in welcome, expectant and willing.

With the night falling around them, Miles felt his heart falling too, and it was an exhilaration like no other. They kissed for long stretches of time, their arms bound around the other, holding one another close. She sighed as the kiss deepened, and Miles let himself get lost in the thrill of the moment.

He couldn't remember being kissed this way, or even if he ever had. To be vulnerable with someone who not only deserved it, but reciprocated it, was a gift Miles had never received, nor given to anyone. He held his emotions close, his heart even closer. But something about Scarlett made him want to loosen that grasp, made him want to open himself up to the possibility of more. To the possibility of falling in love.

That thought struck him hard.

One by one, twinkling stars debuted in the navy sky above and while Miles would have loved nothing more than to stay in the moment with Scarlett, it was nearing Cooper's bedtime. He knew he shouldn't be away much longer.

"We should probably head back," he suggested, even though every ounce of him wanted to keep kissing this incredible woman until sunrise. "I'm sure Levi's ready for a break."

She groaned a little in disappointment. "Do we have to?" Tugging his collar, she drew him close and planted another kiss on his lips. If they continued kissing like teenagers in this way, they would never leave.

"We have to."

She huffed. "I know. Miles, I'm not exaggerating when I say this night has been nothing short of wonderful. The food. The conversation." Her mouth raised up on one side. "The kissing."

"I hope not in that specific order."

"No, not in that order," she said. "Thank you for making me feel like the most special woman in the world."

Miles smiled, beginning to think Scarlett might be exactly that.

CHAPTER TWELVE

*S*carlett spent the next few days managing
the Café from open to close, which left little
time for social activities. Still, Scarlett and Miles
carved out any available minute together that
they could.

They would join each other on a routine trip to
the store, pushing their carts side by side. They'd
wash, sort, and fold Cooper's laundry at the laun-
dromat in town. Scarlett had even invited Miles to go
with her to get her oil changed, a task he offered to do
himself instead. So she played hopscotch with Cooper
on the sidewalk outside the Inn while Miles tinkered
with her sedan in the long driveway and Eugene
looked on from his place in the front porch rocker.

It was truly something special to tag along for
ordinary tasks and yet anticipate the moments as if
they were huge events. That's how life felt with Miles:

big and full. Like Scarlett was experiencing things on a completely new level, seeing with brand new eyes.

Was that what it was like to be in love?

She couldn't say, but she didn't doubt it. It was too soon to know, and even if the brevity of their short relationship wasn't an issue, the fact that Miles was just passing through would be.

They never really talked about his plans to leave, but she knew they weren't concrete. That hope wrapped protectively around her, giving her the assurance that it was okay to open up her heart just a little. And one day when Scarlett walked into the Inn's kitchen after jumping rope outside with Cooper and Miles, she refilled their lemonade glasses from the pitcher in the fridge and Beth confirmed that hunch.

"He's paid several weeks out, you know," she said in passing, but Scarlett didn't miss the knowing glimmer in her eye.

It seemed everyone in Harmony Ridge had some suspicion about Scarlett and Miles. It surprised her how much that didn't even bother her. Not in the least. They could talk all they wanted, and she was fine with that because she wasn't about to deny her feelings. Not to herself. Not to anybody.

Life was too short and happiness too precious to do that.

ON A THURSDAY MORNING, SCARLETT AWOKE TO A text alert on her phone. When she rubbed the sleep from her eyes with a lazy fist, Miles' name snapped into focus.

Any chance you can call in sick tomorrow?

A smile as slow and just as sweet as molasses in January slid across her mouth.

I own the place—I don't have to call in sick. I make the schedule, remember? she typed out.

She rolled over. Light pierced through the parted curtains, swathing the portion of the queen-sized bed where she sprawled. She stretched out like a napping tabby cat to soak up the warmth. Yawning, she lifted the phone closer to read his incoming text.

Cooper and I would like to invite you on a hike through the Ridge. Boots required, costume optional. Your chariot will pick you up at 9:00 AM.

———

Scarlett was a lover of surprises. She could never quite understand how someone could be averse to the idea of them. What was better than being shocked and awed in the best way possible?

When she was just a little girl, she insisted all of her birthday parties be surprise ones, but since she shared her birthdate with Levi—her twin who just so happened to loathe surprises—that wish was fulfilled less than a handful of times.

Like a worker bee in a field of wild poppies, Scarlett felt the buzz of possibility course through her the following morning as she readied herself for her day with Miles and Cooper. The mirror reflected her joy, that wide, shining smile spread so full it almost made putting her lip gloss on a challenge. She couldn't keep from beaming.

There would be some form of hiking involved. Miles indicated she would need the appropriate footwear for that. But that was as much as he'd divulged and it got her mind working overtime, her overactive gears clicking out potential scenarios.

Had he already picked up on her spontaneous nature? He liked to keep her somewhat in the dark when they made plans. Each time they would go out and she would piece things together as the evening unfolded, it was like opening one of those lovely Russian nesting dolls, gift after gift for her to enjoy.

And today's adventure was no exception. Scarlett hurried to get dressed, pulling on her favorite denim jeans along with a burgundy t-shirt that fell loosely below her waistband. The weather in Harmony Ridge had been indecisive, so she tied a lightweight, long-sleeved jacket around her middle for good measure and laced up her hiking boots. It was sunny enough that her fair skin would easily burn, so she fixed her hair into a low ponytail and fit a ball cap onto her head to keep her face shaded.

By nine, she was ready to go, and when she heard Miles' truck ambling up the driveway, her heart clenched within her chest. It had a habit of doing that lately, along with her palms sweating and her knees going weak—every romantic instinct she had always assumed to be fictitious suddenly becoming very real. Her reaction to Miles was strong, both physically and emotionally. She wondered if, over time, all of that might wear off.

But then her memories would scroll back to when her father would glimpse her mother stepping out from their back bedroom, readied for a date wearing a simple black dress and painted red lip, and he would lose all ability to form a coherent sentence.

Even after thirty-five years of marriage, her beauty continued to render him utterly speechless.

That provided Scarlett all the hope she needed—hope that the fleeting infatuation of early dating could one day lead to unconditional love in a lifelong relationship.

Not that she was letting her thoughts leapfrog that many steps forward.

"One day at a time, Scarlett," she cautioned herself aloud as she locked the front door on her way out and tossed her keys into her backpack.

Miles was already out of the truck, moving up the path to greet her. His lips met her cheek as soon as he reached her and she melted into the warmth of his strong body close to hers. He smelled freshly bathed, a minty scent of soap mixed with a musky cologne that blended into an intoxicating aroma she wanted to bottle up and keep.

"Good morning." His voice rasped into her ear.

It would be the only time in their day without Cooper closely in tow, so she took advantage of the moment and pressed her mouth deeply to Miles'.

He kissed her back with fervor.

"It certainly *is* a good morning," she said before pulling out of his arms to walk toward the idling truck. Casting a look over her shoulder, she could see Miles stuck in his tracks, as though the rubber tread of his shoes had melted to the driveway.

"Cooper!" Scarlett half-shouted when she came closer to the vehicle and glimpsed the boy sitting in his booster. "You look amazing, dude!"

Raising his hand up to touch the top of his head, Cooper asked, "You like my bear ears?"

"I do! They look so real!" Of course, they didn't, not really. It was just a headband with two fuzzy little brown ears tacked onto the top, likely part of a costume. But her imagination was big and she could pretend she was seated right next to a grizzly if she pleased.

"Here are yours." He passed off another set of ears to Scarlett.

"I get some too?"

"Yep. And so does Daddy."

Miles climbed back into the truck and shifted out of park. "We all get bear ears because we're…"

"Going on a bear hunt!" Cooper bellowed at the top of his lungs. He waved and waggled Orson directly in front of Scarlett's face.

"We are not!" She played along.

"Yes, we are," Cooper rallied.

"So you must've heard, then?"

"Heard what?" Concern shot across the boy's face.

"That Harmony Ridge is a bear hunting paradise! Would you believe that one day I stumbled on a teddy bear picnic, three bears and a girl with golden hair, *and* a bear with a jar full of honey, all on the same hike?"

"I don't believe it!" Cooper exclaimed.

"I know! I couldn't either. But there's a reason I was able to find all those bears that day."

"There was?"

Scarlett nodded. "Yep. And if you wait here, I'll run inside and get it."

Miles looked at her thoughtfully and shifted the vehicle into park before Scarlett hurried back into the house. It had been years since she'd used them, so she wasn't hopeful she'd find what she was looking for right away. Unused things had a way of disappearing. She knew that. So when she pulled down a dusty box from the uppermost shelf of her linen closet and the item in question was sitting right on top, relief filled her.

"Did you find it? Did you find it?" Cooper hardly waited for the truck door to open to ask. "What is it? What did you get?"

Scarlett withdrew the item from behind her back and draped the strap around Cooper's small neck.

"Binoculars?"

"Oh, these aren't your run-of-the-mill binoculars, Cooper. These are unlike any you've probably ever seen or used."

Over the top of Cooper's head, Scarlett gave Miles an instructive wink to play along. He smiled back as he reversed out of the driveway and onto the road, heading toward their hiking destination.

"These, Cooper, are *bear*-noculars."

"*Bear*-noculars?"

"Yep. They are special binoculars that help you see hidden teddy bears in the forest. They have magical powers."

"They do?"

Scarlett's head lifted in a nod. "They sure do. Only the person using them can see the bears with them. Do you think you'd like to be in charge of them today?"

Brown hair flopped around his face as Cooper nodded rapidly. "I sure would!"

"Great! Then they're all yours. You have to be super careful with them, okay? Remember, they're magic."

"*Bear*-noculars," Cooper repeated under a soft breath, admiring the old set as he turned them over in his small hands. His finger traced one lens, then the next.

They'd been a gift from Scarlett's dad when she was just a little girl, back in the days when they would hike through Harmony Ridge looking for birds and butterflies, sometimes even fairies and sprites. They were clunky and took a bit of work to focus properly, but she wasn't lying about the magic part. She'd felt as though she could see an entirely new world when they were slung around her neck. Of course, she knew her father added a good dose of magic to their adventures, his large tales and huge imagination the biggest transportation device to that realm of make believe.

She hoped with all her heart she'd be able to create a little of that for Cooper today.

CHAPTER THIRTEEN

"There's one!" Cooper had the eyepiece pressed into his sockets as he shouted emphatically, arm flapping about. "I see one!"

"You do? What is he doing?" Scarlett came up behind the boy and crouched down to his level.

"He's swimming," Cooper said, giggling. "And he's wearing floaties. Silly bear."

Miles wasn't far behind. They'd traipsed at least two miles through the ridge surrounding the town, following large fire roads that tapered to smaller offshoots of foot trails meandering through the dense forest. It was beautiful scenery, but the camaraderie forming between Cooper and Scarlett was the most beautiful part of it all.

She was all in. Miles sometimes had to force himself to play along, especially after a big night when he'd left it all out on the stage. He'd have to summon his few remaining dregs of energy for make-believe or bedtime stories, but Scarlett seemed to have no trouble falling right in step with the imaginative adventure. It was inspiring.

"Can I see, bud?" Miles bent low to take in the view from his son's level.

"You won't be able to see them." Cooper thrust his thumb to the middle of his chest. "Just me. I've got the magic *bear*-noculars."

"You do," Scarlett agreed. "But part of the magic is sharing with others, remember?"

Disappointment lowered Cooper's shoulders an inch, and he removed the binoculars from around his neck to pass them off to his dad, huffing a little.

"Oh my goodness," Miles said. "You would not believe this."

"What?" Cooper yanked on his dad's sleeve. "What is it?"

"That bear just did a belly flop!"

"No way!" The young boy scrambled over and pulled at the binoculars, trying to steal a peek for himself. "I wanna see. I wanna see!"

"Look. Right over there." With the strap still around his neck, Miles moved the eyepiece over for Cooper to take in the view. He wrapped his son under his arm and pulled him near. "Do you see it? It's like they're doing some sort of diving competition."

"I see! Oh, that was a *really* big splash."

Under the canopy of trees and covered in the sweetness of the moment, Scarlett looked on, her arms crossed loosely over her chest, her gaze drawn toward the still surface of the pond several yards ahead of them. "Did you feel that?"

The guys spun around.

"I totally felt that splash. Didn't you?"

Cooper shook his head. "I didn't feel it," he said in a tone ripe with utter and complete dejection. He yanked the binoculars from around his dad's neck and fit them back onto his. "There's another bear! Oh, this one is huge!"

"What's he doing?" Scarlett moved closer.

"He's about to do a cannon ball!"

"No way."

"He is!" Cooper's voice lifted with glee. "He really is!"

Miles could hear Scarlett unzip her backpack and when she pulled out her water bottle and unscrewed the cap, he had an idea where she was going with it.

"There he goes!" Cooper said, his voice mounting with expectation. "One, two...three!"

At the last count, Scarlett shook the bottle, dousing them all with a spray of water droplets. In no time flat, she discarded the bottle back to her pack before Cooper could spin around to glimpse it.

"Did you guys feel that?" the boy screamed.

"I did." Miles brushed a drop of water from his eyes with his finger. "We totally got soaked, buddy! That must've been a huge bear."

"The hugest!" Cooper looked up at Scarlett with awe-filled eyes and said, "These *bear*-noculars really *are* magic."

"I told you they were."

The hike only lasted another half hour until Cooper's tiny feet finally gave out and Miles offered to give him a piggyback ride instead. Cooper had asked Scarlett to be in charge of the *bear*-noculars for a bit, and Miles would glimpse her looking through the lenses every now and then out of his periphery.

On their way back to the truck, they stopped at a felled log to take a breather and tear into the snacks Miles had prepared for their journey. They made sandwich crackers with salami and yellow cheese slices for the middles, and drank juice out of boxes. Miles hadn't felt this carefree in years, and he took the quiet moment to appreciate everything about his life that led him to this point in time.

Scarlett sat with Cooper in her lap. She listened with rapt attention to every story he came up with about bugs and bears and the one time he fell and scraped his knee and it bled really badly, but he didn't even cry. Her hand affectionately smoothed down his hair as he spoke. Miles even caught her press a kiss to the back of Cooper's head.

His heart was so full it could split his chest in two.

"Should we pack up and head back into town?" Miles asked once all the snacks had been consumed and stories told. "I think we should squeeze in a nap for you today, Cooper. It's been a big afternoon and you've only been feeling well for a few days."

"I'm too excited from the bear hunt to nap," the boy protested. "I won't be able to sleep. No way."

"Oh, I bet you can." Scarlett squinted knowingly. "You know, bears *love* to sleep."

"They do?"

"Yep. They sleep for entire winters."

"They sleep through Christmas?" Cooper half-shrieked.

"I suppose they do. That's how much they love to sleep."

He shook his head, frowning. "Don't let me sleep through Christmas."

"I won't, buddy," Miles assured. "I won't."

BEFORE THEY'D EVEN PULLED ONTO THE HIGHWAY back into town, Cooper was out cold in his booster seat, his little snores a soft soundtrack for their ride.

"It was a big day for him." Miles glanced over at Scarlett on the other side of the cab. "I'm surprised he made it this long without crashing."

"He's a really special kid, Miles. You should be proud."

"Not sure I have much to do with it, but thank you."

"You have everything to do with it."

He didn't know how to receive the compliment, so he just let it sit. "Thank you for coming with us today. What I had planned was nothing compared to what you were able to pull off."

"We make a good team," she said. He would've

reached out to hold her hand had Cooper's booster seat not been wedged between them.

It was funny, really. Sometimes he thought having a child might get in the way of meeting someone. That didn't seem to be the case with Scarlett, and other than his son physically keeping Miles from holding her hand at the moment, Cooper didn't get in the way one bit.

Miles couldn't let his heart go there, but this was the closest to having a little family that they'd ever gotten.

"When can we do this again?" Miles asked.

"Another bear hunt? Oh goodness, I think I need to recover from this one for a few days. You weren't kidding when you said I would need hiking boots. I almost asked you to carry me that last stretch of the way before Cooper snagged the spot in your arms first."

"I would have gladly carried you," Miles said, his voice more playful than usual. He enjoyed flirting with Scarlett; she made it so fun and easy, these back-and-forth hints of affection.

"Then maybe we *should* go hiking again," she rallied. "But seriously, I would love to spend more time with the two of you. I just need to work things out at the Café."

For an instant, guilt wove through him. He'd kept her away from her job all day long, and while he knew everyone deserved time off, the Café was Scarlett's everything. It felt almost unfair to pull her away from her responsibilities there.

"You know, I'm actually thinking of scaling back our hours."

He didn't like the sound of that. "Really? Why?"

"The numbers aren't where they need to be. I think if we just serve breakfast and lunch, the operational costs I'll save might even things out a bit. That's the hope, at least."

The stoplight ahead morphed from yellow to red, and Miles eased off the gas and pressed his foot to the brakes to come to a full stop. When he did, he took the moment to look over at Scarlett.

"When I came by the other night before our date, the place was packed. Not a vacant seat in the house. You don't think you can capitalize on that evening rush?"

"If everyone paid full price, I'm sure I could. But that's just not the case anymore."

He didn't follow. "Scarlett, why isn't everyone paying full price?"

She took a breath, then smoothed out her composure at the same time as she smoothed her palms over her pant legs. "The prices on the menu are more like suggestions."

"Suggestions?"

"If someone can't pay their full bill, we make it work. And we've always had no trouble making it work. Until recently. I think maybe the word got out about the whole *'pay what you can'* thing, because in the last couple of weeks, we've had a lot more patrons only footing small portions of their bill. But, like I said, we'll make it work. Always do."

Miles still didn't understand. "Why would your community want to take advantage of you like that? By the looks of all the manicured yards and expensive vehicles, most people around here can easily afford to pay for their meals."

"Oh, it's not really the locals. I mean, sometimes I comp Eugene's meals, and of course my brother gets to eat for free—"

"Sure, but that's your choice to gift them those meals," Miles said. "Where are these other people even coming from?"

"We get a lot of travelers passing through, like you and Cooper. We're one of the only food stops in the area, so travelers come in for a warm breakfast or bowl of soup. Up until recently, these patrons kept the Café going. I'm just not sure how they found out about Dad's legacy of only having his customers pay what they were able."

"Scarlett, you have to know that your dad wouldn't want you to keep that tradition going if it was about to run the place into the ground."

Her eyes went cold and the smile that had been a permanent fixture slipped from her face. "I don't think being generous is ever a bad thing," she said firmly.

"No, I know it's not. And I didn't mean to upset—"

"I'm not upset," she cut him off, but her voice betrayed her. "Anyway, I shouldn't have said anything. It's my problem to work out. You don't need to worry about it."

He wanted to say more, but his sister had taught him long ago that sometimes a woman just wanted to discuss her problems, not necessarily have them fixed. It was like torture to keep from looking for ways to solve this specific issue, but he let it be and for the rest of the drive, they sat quietly.

He'd upset her whether she would admit to it or not, and that was the last possible way he wanted to end their day together.

When they pulled up to Scarlett's house, silence still thick around them, Miles walked her to the door. He was ready to go in for a kiss when she intercepted the moment with a hug and a brief "thank you" for the lovely day.

The formality of it all made Miles' heart plummet to his toes, but she was in the house and shutting the door before he even had the chance to apologize for his blunder.

CHAPTER FOURTEEN

$\mathcal{I}$t was still dark out when Scarlett pulled up to the Campfire Café. As usual, there was a line of cars along the curb with engines idling, waiting for the CLOSED sign to flip around to OPEN. These patrons commuted to Hamilton, the closest metropolitan city, about an hour outside of Harmony Ridge. They typically ordered a cup of coffee and a breakfast sandwich or burrito to go, and Scarlett had always been so grateful for their consistent patronage.

Especially today. She needed those counted on dollars in the cash register.

With her purse jammed under her arm and the keys in the deadbolt, she opened the door to the restaurant and locked it shut behind her. In twenty minutes, the rush would begin, but she took this moment of calm to gather herself.

Miles had undoubtedly rattled her the night

before. She couldn't understand why it bothered her as much as it did. She couldn't expect him to understand the meaning of this place and her role in keeping it going. He was an outsider. That wasn't his fault, but it meant he wasn't as entrenched in the goings-on of Harmony Ridge as she was. For goodness' sake, her last name was Harmony, after all. This town and this Café meant the world to her. They *were* her whole world.

And it never crossed her mind that closing the doors of the Café was even a possibility. Not until the last week or so when the dismal numbers forced her thoughts in a direction she'd never let them travel.

Things were in a steady decline, and something needed to be done.

"Morning, Dom," she said, entering the kitchen where her head chef was already busy preparing for the day. He had prepping bowls and colorful, freshly chopped ingredients lining the long table, all set for the recipes he would spend his morning concocting.

"Hey there, Scarlett. You have fun yesterday?"

It had been more than fun. It was perfect, even. Until that car ride home where she had opened up and then completely *clammed* up.

"It was great," was all she said, worried that if she got into it, she'd get worked up all over again. She didn't have time for that. Not today. She needed to focus on other things. "How did we do yesterday?"

He just gave her a somber look, and that was all she needed to read the situation.

"That bad?"

Dominic put both large hands on the stainless table between them, his stance squared off. "We're not a soup kitchen, Scarlett. I understand where your heart is in this, but it's not what your dad would have wanted."

"You don't know what my dad would've wanted."

The look he gave Scarlett exposed the lie in that statement. "You serious right now? Before I ever wore this chef's apron, it was *my* father who wore it. Are you forgetting that our dads were originally in this together?"

Dominic's father had been her dad's closest friend. He was like an uncle to Scarlett and Levi. She hadn't meant to insult Dom, but she could clearly see the damage in his eyes. "I'm so sorry. I know. This place means a lot to you too."

"It does. And you mean a lot, which is why I hate to see you so upset by the state of things. I don't think it's unreasonable to start demanding that people pay their full share. Last time I checked, this was a business. *Your* business."

Her lips pressed into a line. "I just don't understand the uptick in freebies. Before, we'd get a couple of people a week that couldn't pay their tab and that wasn't an issue at all. But now, entire reservations are completely skipping out without even tossing a few dollars onto the table."

"I don't get it, either. But you know I'll support whatever you choose to do. I'm in this with you, one-hundred percent." Dom tightened his apron around his waist. "Hey, I forgot to tell you I was able to head into Hamilton to purchase some of the items in bulk that we needed for this week, so that should shave off some of the overhead."

"You didn't buy local?" Dominic always bought his ingredients locally.

"Scarlett, you know how expensive that can be. I'm just trying to help us stay afloat."

She took a solid breath. "I know. I'm sorry. I'm grateful for you, Dom, and I trust you to run the kitchen. Do whatever it takes to cut back on costs for now and we'll make this thing work. We have to."

By the time the Café was ready to open, Scarlett had given herself a thorough pep talk, pasted on a smile, and pushed her worries to the back of her mind.

Familiar faces greeted her throughout the day and ordered their favorite menu items. Eugene and Lottie stopped in, and the two shared the same side of the booth and one milkshake with two straws.

It was busy, which Scarlett was grateful for, but she found herself distracted. With each group that passed through, she would total up their bill in her head and keep her fingers crossed they would pay even a small portion of it.

By the end of the day, exhaustion got the better of her and the burden of worry had made her weary. She slumped into a corner booth to look at the numbers, her brain as frazzled as a fraying knot.

Dominic joined her. He handed her a mug of hot chocolate with three jumbo marshmallows, just the way she liked it.

"How'd we do?"

"Better," she said, which was encouraging. She took a slow sip of the warm drink and felt the heat trickle all the way down to her stomach. "But we have a way to go."

"You have a good heart, Scarlett. I totally get what you're doing with your dad's legacy here." Dominic had a Thermos of coffee in his hands and he wrapped his fingers around the stainless cup, leaning his head a little as he searched her out from across the table. "But you have a legacy too. Don't forget that. I know your dad opened up this place, but you don't want to be the one to close it."

Dominic's unstripped words settled into her heart that night as Scarlett mindlessly watched a documentary on penguins, curled up on the couch in her pajamas with a bottle of wine that had been in her cupboard for years.

Would that be her legacy? If she couldn't keep the Café up and running, would she ultimately be remembered as the daughter who couldn't keep her father's dream alive?

Her heart dropped, a wave of fresh grief rushing over her.

She couldn't let the Café close down. It wasn't an

option. She'd lost her father once already, and losing the Café would feel like a whole new tragedy, one she wasn't sure she could endure.

She sat for so long, lost in her thoughts, that she didn't even notice the credits rolling at the end of the show until the screen went entirely black. Swathed in darkness, she fumbled for the remote, only locating it after a long search that resulted in removing the couch cushions to find the missing device. Why was she suddenly so scattered in all areas of her life?

Taking her empty wineglass with her to the kitchen, she gave it a rinse in the sink and left it at the edge of the counter. Her hands bracketed the sink's ledge, holding her steady.

She hated this melancholy that weighted her stomach. She wasn't like this—so glum and miserable. Scarlett had always been a glass half full kind of person, but right now the glass felt bone dry.

If she were honest with herself, a lot of the sadness was about the dire straits of the Café, but a good portion stemmed from the way she'd left things with Miles. She hated how cold she had been. How she'd closed him off the moment he questioned her judgment about the way she ran her business. Why had she taken it so personally? She couldn't make sense of it and that was a frustration that ate away at her.

She should have valued Miles' opinion, not been threatened by it. While they hadn't talked in twenty-four hours, it felt like weeks. And that was crazy because they'd barely known one another that long.

How had he so quickly slipped into her life and made himself a permanent fixture?

And what if he slipped back out just as quickly? Would Scarlett be able to live with that regret?

CHAPTER FIFTEEN

*J*f Miles could be grateful for only one thing at the Inn, it would be the full bath, equipped with a cast-iron tub that his son would go straight into once they finished up their morning at the community garden. The child not only had dirt up to his elbows, but clear up into his armpits. Not that digging in the soil for overwintered potatoes could result in anything much different. Even Miles had a good layer of dirt coating his sweat-slicked skin, like two sleeves made from soil. He shook out his arms, but the grime stayed put.

"How're you boys doing?" Pearl notched the brim of her wide straw hat up higher onto her forehead and hovered over the father and son working busily in the planter boxes. "Finding any leftover taters in there?"

"I found four and Daddy found three!" Cooper

shook the tubers in his metal bucket. "But I think that's all."

"Good job, boys." Tugging the knees of her pants, Pearl squatted down with a grunt. "Now that those are out of there, we can use this bed to grow something else."

"What are we gonna grow?" Cooper asked.

Miles would've winced at the way his son pressed his filthy palms to Pearl's thigh to snuggle in close had she not wrapped her own arm around his shoulder, swallowing his affection.

"Well, we're going to grow tomatoes in this box. The big heirloom kind that you can cut in fat, juicy slices. Perfect for hamburgers and sandwiches on a hot summer's day."

"Potato, tomato." Cooper threw his head back with a laugh. "Those rhyme."

"Sure do. Just like seed and weed. And sow and grow." She gave Cooper a little pat on his back, encouraging him off of her knee as she stood up. "You know, I often say you can learn more in the great outdoors than you can in any classroom."

She'd lost Cooper at that point, the child now distracted by a monarch butterfly that zigzagged as it fluttered from plant to plant in his periphery. She turned to Miles.

"I like to think of this here community garden as a place that not only nourishes the body but also the mind."

Miles almost added the soul to the list. It had done

wonders for his. What was once preoccupied over the tension with Scarlett now felt significantly lighter, as though the thirsty ground soaked up his worries like a fresh spring rain.

"Cooper, you want to give me a hand with the fertilizer bags? They're too heavy for me to carry on my own. You think you could help out?"

Making muscles by lifting his arms to flex by his ears, Cooper roared, "I'm super-duper strong! I can help you."

"Well, that's perfect. And Miles? If you want to head over to the potting shed at the north side of the garden, I think my son, J.P., could use a hand replacing the roof. The shingles just came in today and I'd like to get it put up before the rain that's expected this weekend."

"I don't have a lot of construction experience, but I'm happy to learn."

"J.P.'s a builder. He'll tell you what to do, how to do it, and he'll also tell you how you're doing it wrong. But take that last part with a grain of salt. He likes to think he's the only person who knows how to use a hammer around here. Confidence isn't an issue for him, but I'm sure he'd appreciate the help, even if he's not agreeable to it right off the bat."

Several parts of that statement intimidated Miles, and when he made his way over to the shed and saw the job he'd been tasked to, that intimidation morphed into all-out overwhelm.

"My mom send you over?" Straddling the pitch of

the roof with one leg on either side of the sloping eaves, a man looking to be in his mid-twenties spoke around a nail pinned between his front teeth. He popped the small spike from his mouth and whacked it into a board with the flat head of his hammer.

"She did. I'm Miles."

"You know how to install a roof?"

"I don't."

It was as though he was admitting he didn't know how to recite his *ABC's*. J.P. glowered at him from his lofty vantage point. "You ever build anything?"

"Does assembling a nightstand from IKEA count?"

A raspy laugh tore from J.P.'s lips. "Those suckers are challenging. You get some credit there. Grab a hammer."

You would've thought Miles had won the approval of the Pope, he was so delighted by J.P.'s comment. He gathered the hammer from the toolbox on the potting table nearby, then scaled the first few rungs of the ladder. By the fourth, his legs felt weak. By the fifth, he was completely boneless, clinging to the metal ladder for the dear life he was certain would be cut short if he scaled another step.

"You afraid of heights, boss?"

"Not necessarily afraid. I just have a healthy respect for gravity."

J.P. fit his hammer into a loop on his leather tool belt and clapped his hands to his legs. "If you think about gravity when you're up here, it's a surefire bet that you'll end up on the wrong side of it. Don't think."

"How do I not think?"

"Do you think about putting one foot in front of the other when you're walking down the street?"

No, Miles supposed he didn't. He shook his head, but even that slight movement was enough to wobble the ladder and the confidence right out of him.

"Just do it. Some things in this life come naturally."

Scaling a ladder to sit on a roof felt as natural as voluntarily hugging a porcupine, but he had a feeling J.P. wasn't going to let him off the hook now. What had happened to Pearl saying he might outright refuse the help?

"C'mon, boss. You got this."

Miles so did not have this.

"You got a lady?"

"Huh?"

Even at a distance, Miles could detect the eye roll. "You got a lady? A girlfriend?"

Well, that wasn't a one-word-answer type of question when it came to the situation with Scarlett. In the time it took Miles to arrange his words, J.P. had already blown right past the original question.

"Just think about her being up here. You gotta get to her. Nothing else matters."

Yeah, that wasn't going to help. If Scarlett had been on top of a roof, Miles would've preferred she come down, not that he go up.

And maybe that was the entire problem with it all. Miles had suggested Scarlett change things at the Café rather than just listen to her and consider the way she wanted to run her business. He'd asked her to come down rather than climb up to see things from her perspective.

"You solving the world's problems down there, boss?" J.P.'s shout wrenched Miles from his thoughts.

"No, just trying to work up the courage to take another step."

"I don't have all day and I'm running out of pep talks. If you want to help, help. If you don't, don't. You make the call. But in the meantime, I've got a roof to shingle."

Miles *had* wanted to help. He wanted to give back to Pearl, give back to the community that he already felt so much a part of. Swallowing his fear behind an embarrassingly audible gulp, Miles closed his eyes and raised a leg to ascend another rung.

"Whoa!" J.P. screamed. "What are you doing?"

Miles' eyes flew open. "I'm coming up there to help you."

"Not with your eyes closed, you're not. Listen, I get that this is scary for you, but sometimes you gotta do the scary stuff with your eyes wide open. Climbing a ladder and scaling a roof fall into that category." Swinging a leg over the ridge, J.P. popped up to his feet and jogged—*jogged*—down the slope of the roof. "Grab my hand."

Like he'd been flung a life saver in shark-infested

waters, Miles took J.P.'s hand into his grip and let the man hoist him the last of the way up and onto the roof.

"Keep your feet flat and walk sideways." He lifted a hand to pat Miles on the back, then likely thought better of it. "And don't look down. If you need to look somewhere, keep your eyes on the horizon."

It was the advice he'd tried to follow on this journey: keeping his focus in front of him and letting his past stay in the rearview.

And when he looked toward that horizon now and the future laid out for him, he envisioned Scarlett. Funnily enough, being around her felt a lot like falling —scary, but in the very best way possible, and with his eyes wide open to the risks and rewards of every single step.

CHAPTER SIXTEEN

"Can you pass me another mason jar?" Scarlett secured her fingers around the flower stems like a makeshift rubber band.

Stretching over the lavender row between them, Chloe pulled out another jar from the wooden crate and passed it off. "How many do you think we should make?"

"One for each table at the Café, four for the bar, and one for my kitchen island." She needed the cheery presence of flowers to perk up her home and her mood. "If we make twenty, we should be good."

Spending time in Beth's garden with flowers and friends was the ideal prescription for Scarlett's melancholy mood. She'd tried everything to keep her thoughts from traveling back to the day she'd spent with Miles in this very place. That first time he'd held her hand and held her heart within his own. She had spent countless afternoons tending to the flowers here, each providing memories that didn't have Miles in the very center.

And yet, when she tried to lock in on those, they were fuzzy, like a television channel out of reception. Why was it that Miles was the only clear memory? How was it that he chased away all other thoughts, save for the ones involving him? It was like some unfair mind game, this insistence that he was front and center.

In truth, Scarlett only had herself to blame. It wasn't as though Miles had been pestering her. She'd heard stories of men sending text after text following an argument, phone call after insistent phone call. Since their discussion, Miles hadn't even attempted to contact her.

And it had been an argument, hadn't it? Scarlett wasn't even sure anymore. If pressed, she would have to admit that she hadn't given him any time to argue—no time to say his piece. She'd just shut the door and locked him out, both physically and metaphorically.

"Earth to Scarlett?" Chloe shook a handful of lavender at her friend, small, dried blooms shuddering off the plant like pastel purple snowflakes. "You lost up in there?"

"Do you and Levi ever argue?"

"Oh." Chloe's chin pulled back. "Sure. Of course, we've had our disagreements."

"And what sorts of things do you disagree on?"

Lowering the bunch of stems to the ledge of the

planter, Chloe clasped her hands together and leaned forward on her gardening stool, meeting Scarlett's eye over the flowers between them. "It's not so much that there's a list of things we disagree on. Just that sometimes things will come up that we need to work through. Together."

"And how do you work through them?" Needing to busy her hands as much as her mind, Scarlett picked up a pair of shears and cut the healthy stalks of lavender from the plant directly in front of her.

Brown waves brushing over her shoulders, Chloe waggled her head. "Every disagreement is different, but Levi is the same. I've learned how to communicate with him. How he responds to feedback and how he hears me. How he interprets my feelings."

"And this is where I have no experience."

"Sure you do."

Taking the empty jar, Scarlett crammed the flowers into it, instantly feeling guilty for the unnecessary roughness she inflicted on the innocent blooms. "Is there some period of time where I had amnesia that I don't know about? Because I don't remember ever being in a relationship."

"Maybe not a romantic one, but all relationships require work." Chloe's gaze softened. "Remember back in the fifth grade when I was invited to Rebecca's ice skating party, and you weren't?"

"How can I forget? I was the only girl in the class who even knew how to ice skate and she conveniently left me off of the guest list."

"Remember how mad you were at me? How I tried explaining that it wasn't my fault that I'd been invited—that I hadn't asked to be. Remember that I even had our moms schedule our own special trip to Harmony Ridge Pond for an afternoon of ice skating, just you and me?"

"Oh, I remember." Scarlett fiddled with the petals, the shame from the adolescent memory socking her in the stomach with regret. "I remember what a terrible friend I was and how I told you I didn't need your sympathy skating. Super mature of me."

"I was just trying to fix the problem."

"But it wasn't even your problem to begin with. It was all mine."

Chloe smiled. "I know. But that didn't mean I didn't want to help. That I didn't want to make things better for you."

Slumping down like a sunflower wilting under hot summer temperatures, Scarlett groaned audibly. "You know what? I haven't really matured at all in the last fifteen years."

"Oh, sure you have, Scarlett."

"Not really. I'm reacting the same way I did back then. Punishing the people who only want what's best for me."

"By people, are we referring to Miles?"

Scarlett gave an impish grin. "Sometimes I wonder if I'm even cut out for a relationship."

"Of course you are."

"You so sure? I mean, I meet this great guy, and the moment he offers me advice, I run for the hills."

"You're independent, Scarlett. That's not a bad thing."

"I just wonder if I'll ever get to the point where I'm willing to depend on someone or something other than myself."

Chloe sighed slowly through her mouth. "I don't think it's so much depending on someone. It's more like you want to partner with them. Share the burden, share the responsibility. Share life."

"Hard to partner with a person when they have plans to leave town."

"I don't know about that." A knowing glint came to Chloe's hazel eyes. "If I've learned anything about love, it's that it often does all it takes to stick around."

Scarlett knew the words were meant as a comfort, but she couldn't help but feel suddenly thrown off kilter by them. Even if her heart said she was ready to open herself up in that way, her head was still ten paces—or maybe even miles—back.

CHAPTER SEVENTEEN

"*L*ook how high I am!"

Miles' gaze flicked up from his phone to see Cooper cresting skyward on the swing, his little legs pumping furiously to launch him still higher than the last push.

"Wow, buddy! You're almost up in the trees!" The morning sun glistened and filtered through the branches like a kaleidoscope of white light. Miles shaded his brow against the glare and rested in the warmth.

They had just finished up storytime at the library and stopped by the park on their short walk back to the Inn. It was busy today. It looked like many of the other moms and young children from the library had the same idea for the little ones to stretch their legs and get their wiggles out.

Cooper had waited patiently for his turn on the swings and Miles would check his watch now and then to make sure his son wasn't hogging the popular playground structure. Was there an etiquette about such things? How long was a typical turn on a swing? Miles figured five minutes was a safe bet, so when that rolled around, he told Cooper it was time to get down to let another child have a turn.

It took some time for Cooper to decelerate, and when his sneakered feet skidded to a stop in the sand, he launched from the swing and bounded over to Miles. "Daddy, look at that kid. He still needs his mommy to push him on the swing."

"Most kids your age do, Coop, and there's nothing wrong with that."

"I must have superpowers, because I don't need your help at all." Cooper flung his arms out behind him like a cape and buzzed around Miles in a tight circle.

"It's all those veggies you eat."

"Veggies don't give you super powers. They give you toots!"

"Who told you that?" Miles chuckled.

"Eugene. He said broccoli gives him gas."

Miles had no answer for that. "Eugene is funny."

"What are we going to do today?" Cooper ping-ponged the subject. "I want to see the doggies again."

"At the shelter?"

"Yeah. Remember when we did that after storytime?"

"I remember." He looked at the time on his

phone. "I bet we can make it over there today if we hurry."

"We can make it," Cooper assured. "I have super powers!"

They stopped by the Inn to grab Miles' guitar and then walked the five blocks to the animal shelter, entering the doors just as the head volunteer wrapped up with instructions.

"Nice to see you two again," he acknowledged as the crowd thinned and Miles and Cooper came into view. The man still had Seymour, the one-eyed, half-tailed cat, draped across his shoulders like a scarf. Miles wondered if the cat was actually even up for adoption. The two seemed to have quite an unbreakable bond. "Scarlett's with the large breed animals, if you're looking for her."

Miles hadn't been. Not intentionally, at least. But his heart tripped a little at the information.

"Let's go see the big doggies!" Cooper exclaimed, and he was off like a shot before Miles could stop him.

With his guitar case in his grip, Miles set out after Cooper, weaving his way through the rows of kennels until he could hear his son's joyous squeals increasing in volume.

He turned the corner, just as the boy was about to ambush Scarlett with a hug that was more like a tackle. She was sitting cross-legged on the floor in front of Waylon with a book in her hands, and the force of the embrace rocked her back completely when Cooper made contact.

"Scarlett!" Cooper flung his arms around her neck and squeezed. "Daddy and I went to storytime and then to the park and I was the only kid my age to go on the swing without help. I didn't need anyone to push me."

"Because your legs are so strong from all that walking on our hike," she said, but she spoke only to Cooper and her eyes had yet to meet Miles'.

"What are you reading?" Cooper wiggled around to look at the book Scarlett had been holding.

"Just something I picked up from the library, but I don't think he likes it." She moved her eyes toward the sad-looking dog, curled in a hopeless heap.

"He doesn't like books," Cooper said. "He only likes when Daddy plays the guitar."

She couldn't avoid eye contact any longer without it feeling totally intentional, so Miles was relieved when her eyes finally reached his.

"Hey," he said quietly, but even that word felt like an intrusion. She hadn't wanted him there—or at least hadn't anticipated him being there—and he wondered if it had been a bad idea to come to the shelter after all.

"Hi," she responded. It wasn't much, but Miles would take it.

He thought she'd been mad at him, but a closer look at the sorrow that tugged at her features made him realize she'd been hurt by him. And those were two entirely different things.

"We can go if you and Waylon already have something going," Miles offered. "I don't think there are any volunteers currently reading to the smaller dogs. Coop, want to head over that way? I saw a Chihuahua that looked like he could use a friend."

"Nope." The boy had already made himself comfortable in Scarlett's lap. "I want to stay here with Scarlett and Waylon."

Miles looked at Scarlett.

"It's fine," she said.

He would take her at her word, even though her expression read entirely differently.

Joining them on the cold, concrete floor, Miles slid his guitar out of its case and lowered the strap onto his neck. A few of the dogs from last time were gone. In their place were new pups with the same scared faces and trembling limbs. There was some joy in knowing the others had been adopted, but it was a sad reality that the kennels were filled right back up with newly abandoned pups, just as desperate for loving homes.

"What do you think he'd like to hear?" Miles asked Cooper.

"The one you wrote about me! The one that goes like this." Cooper made little humming noises, off-key and off-beat. "That's my favorite."

"Oh yeah? You think he'd like that one?"

Miles drew a pick from his pocket and placed it

in between his front teeth while his fingers found the chords. It had been a long time since he'd strummed this particular piece. It wasn't one they'd recorded on their album, so it got little play time, other than on nights when Cooper would request it as a playful lullaby, which he didn't seem to do much of anymore.

Still, it came back to Miles like a memory. He didn't sing the words, but hummed them softly and even Cooper joined in. It was a sweet little melody, with a lively and energetic beat you couldn't help but tap your feet to.

Or wag your tail, as was the case for Waylon. The dog swished his long, gray tail along the cement floor, sweeping it back and forth like a hairy mop.

"He likes it!" Cooper jumped from Scarlett's lap and, within seconds, was at the gate to Waylon's kennel. "Keep playing, Daddy. He likes this song."

Miles repeated the last few lines and started back from the top. There was an inherent rhythm and Scarlett found it with her hands, clapping in time with the spirited sound.

Before long, even Waylon was on his feet and that tail swish morphed into a whole body wiggle. Waylon was a tough crowd to please, and his approval made Miles feel something.

It was an infectious tune. Miles always knew that, and at the moment, it was as though it held a bit of magic in those chords too. He didn't want it to end, but he also didn't want to wear it out. Finally, Miles strummed the last note, letting the sound hang in the air around them.

"I think that's Waylon's favorite song," Cooper said. He'd threaded his fingers into the chain link and Waylon's flat tongue licked the boy's hand.

"I think it is too," Miles agreed. He moved his guitar back into its case and ventured a look in Scarlett's direction. "What do you say we let Scarlett have some time to herself with the dogs?"

"No, Miles," she said firmly. "It's fine."

He was so new to this; navigating the emotions of a relationship. Not that they even had a relationship. But there was something between them, and right then it felt as though that something was a huge, immovable wedge.

Scarlett picked up a new book from her stack and led Cooper by the hand toward the kennels at the back of the row. They flipped through the pages together as they read and Scarlett would lift the book to show the pictures to the dogs and to Cooper, who sat pressed up against the kennel gates to be as close to the animals as he could.

A half hour later, when reading time was over, the three packed up their things and set out for the parking lot.

Miles needed to talk to Scarlett. He didn't like the strain between them, and yet he had no clue how to lessen it.

Once Cooper was strapped into his seat, Miles shut the truck door and turned toward Scarlett.

Her eyes were hopeful for a moment, then that sad countenance washed over her again. She gripped her elbows by her sides.

"Hey," Miles said, his voice barely above a whisper. "What's going on, Scarlett? Are you okay?"

She looked like she might cry. "I'm fine, Miles."

"You don't look fine."

She moved her hand to her eyes and wiped. He couldn't see a tear, but if there had been one, she obviously hadn't wanted him to notice it, either.

"I'm really sorry about the way things ended the other day," he said. "I had such a great time and thought things were going so well, but obviously something shifted and all of that changed."

"It's not your fault, Miles. I have a lot going on right now."

"But I obviously said something to bother you. I'm sorry about that."

She sighed, her gaze falling to her feet. "I just don't think this is going to work between us."

Miles bristled. "What?"

"You're just passing through and I've got so much to figure out with the Café. I don't have time to figure this out too." She moved her hands in the space between them.

"We don't have to figure out anything between us. We can just see where it goes. Play it by ear."

She let out a breath that sputtered her lips. "I like you, Miles. I do. More than I probably should. But I don't want to invest in something that can't go anywhere. I don't have the capacity for that right now."

"Why can't this go anywhere?"

"Because you said yourself that you're on a journey. You and Cooper. Out on an adventure. And I think that's great," she said. "But I don't want to just be part of someone's journey. I don't have time for that."

He didn't know how to respond, or if it was even okay to.

Things had happened so quickly between them. Maybe this was just her knee-jerk reaction to that. Maybe all they needed to do was slow things down. Take a step back. Ease off the gas a bit.

"I hear all of that and in my head it makes sense," he said. "But not in my heart."

Her lips slipped into a frown. "I know. I feel the same. But I have to think with my head and not my heart right now. And honestly, I think some of what's going on with the Café is because I haven't had my head in that game at all lately. I've been so preoccupied with you and my feelings for you that I haven't had my head on straight. And that's not like me. I give my all to the things I do. One-hundred percent. And I just can't give one-hundred percent to both you and the restaurant. Something has to give. I'm sorry, but it has to be this." Her hand moved again to indicate the space between them.

"There has to be a way to make both things work: the Café and us."

"There isn't really an us, Miles," she said. "We both know it's too soon for that."

Sure, on paper it was too soon. But life didn't play itself out on paper. It played itself out in small moments of connection. In stolen glances and in fluttering hearts and simple times that made you lose your breath all the same.

He respected Scarlett's position, but he didn't agree with it. And he certainly didn't know what to do with it.

"Can I at least call you? Maybe tonight, after you get off work?"

"I really don't want to rehash all of this," she admitted, her tone and demeanor exasperated.

"I get that. So maybe we don't rehash it. Maybe we rework it."

"How is that any different?"

"Just let me call you and we can see."

Her mouth lifted just a touch, and she nodded. "Okay."

CHAPTER EIGHTEEN

*S*carlett wasn't the type of girl to wait by the
phone, but she did exactly that once she'd
gotten home from the Café and settled into her
evening. She'd showered, reveling in the warm spray
of water as it soaked her hair and loosened her tired
muscles. She always carried her stress in her shoulders, so she took the extra time to let the water raining
down from the showerhead slowly dissolve the day's
worries. Once the water started to run cold, she
figured it was finally time to get out.

Her favorite pajama bottoms were in the hamper,
so she pulled on a pair of loose shorts and fitted an
old college sweatshirt on top, then wrapped her hair
in a loose bun to air dry.

The days were getting longer as spring stretched
into summer, so she poured herself a glass of
sparkling white wine and walked out to her back deck
to soak in the last dregs of the day. Her townhome

was small and her yard even smaller, but she was grateful for the space she could call her own. And the view that came with it couldn't be beat.

Perched at the top of the ridge, from her house, she could take in all of the valley and her beloved community in one sweeping glance. There was something reassuring about this vantage point, like she could keep Harmony Ridge under her watchful gaze and protection. It was silly; she knew that. She didn't have any sort of power to do that, but she felt a responsibility to this town she couldn't shake.

Miles called just as he said he would, and even though she had expected it, something a lot like nerves bolted through her stomach when her phone trilled in her palm.

"Hey," he said when she answered. She could tell by his tone that he wanted to say more, but out of caution, he kept the greeting simple.

"Hi, Miles." Scarlett pressed her phone between her ear and shoulder and topped off her glass from the bottle resting on the bistro table beside her. "How are you?"

"I'm good," he said. "Finally got Cooper down for the night and then went downstairs for Beth's version of a happy hour at the Inn. She had some fancy wine she'd been saving from a trip to France and she wanted to share it with her guests. So I stayed for a bit, did the whole obligatory small talk thing, and brought the rest of my glass back up to the room. I'm no sommelier, but it's not half-bad."

"But is it half-good?"

"That's debatable."

"I'm actually enjoying a glass of wine myself."

"Hey, looks like we're having a drink together then," he said, a little forced chuckle punctuated at the end.

Their conversation was so stilted that Scarlett was grateful they were on the phone and not in person. She hated how awkward things had suddenly become. Being face to face would only intensify that.

"Listen, Scarlett," Miles said. "I think this might be the whole problem."

"What's that?"

"That we're only just now sharing a drink together. I mean, sure, we had a glass of wine on our date at the farmers' market, but we also shared an entire evening and more than a few kisses. We kind of just dove right into things, so I get why you're backing away from that now. It was a lot. For me, too."

She didn't know if that was the real reason for her hesitancy. Sure, their attraction had been instant and their feelings swift, but was that wrong? Wasn't that how people always described meeting someone special? When you knew, you knew? Things just clicked and all of that?

"What I'm trying to say is,"—he continued —"that maybe we should just slow things down a little. Date. Get to know each other better. Go out for a drink together. Talk."

"I'm just not even sure I have time to date, Miles.

The Café is taking everything out of me right now, monetarily and emotionally."

"Then let me help you with that burden," he said.

"Why would you want to do that?"

There was a pause and she could hear him inhale shallowly through the line. "Because what I feel when I'm with you—I don't want to lose that, Scarlett. To be honest, I've never felt so comfortable with someone so quickly before. And Cooper?"

Just saying the boy's name awakened some maternal instinct within Scarlett that she never even realized she possessed. It was fair to say that little guy had quickly wrapped her entirely around his little finger.

"Cooper loves you," he went on to say.

"Kids get attached easily," she offered weakly.

"Sure, they can. But Cooper has been around a lot of adults in his short life on the road with me. And I can honestly say he hasn't bonded with anyone as fast as he has with you. It's different."

She didn't want to hear that. It made her determination to give Miles and Cooper space all the more difficult to cling to.

"I don't know what to do with this, Miles."

"Am I crazy in thinking the feelings I have for you aren't one-sided?" His voice held equal amounts of hope and hesitation. "You feel it too, don't you? Or am I imagining all of this?"

"Of course, I do. I feel it. But I'm really not

prepared to give you my heart and then have you leave town with it."

There was a pause and Scarlett could hear her erratic pulse thrumming loudly in her ears as she waited for his reply. Why had she confessed that?

"Maybe I don't have to leave town."

"What do you mean by that?"

"I don't know. I mean, Cooper and I set out to find some stability, but I'm beginning to think that only comes when you put down roots. As long as we're on the road, things are going to be just as tumultuous as they were when I was with the band. We still won't be settled."

"I can't ask you to stay in Harmony Ridge just to see if things can work between us. That's not fair to either of you."

"But why isn't it? How will we know if we've found home unless we let ourselves *make* a home exactly where we are?" It felt almost rhetorical. "And Scarlett, I've never felt more at home than when I'm with you."

It might've been the wine, but that confession made her toes tingle and her stomach drift instantly weightless. "So what do we do?" she asked, her voice uncharacteristically unsure.

"I can see if Beth can let us stay here through the end of the month. That gives us three solid weeks. I think that's more than enough time to see if Harmony Ridge is where we should dig some roots and plant some dreams."

Her heart swelled at the beautiful words—the words of a gifted songwriter—and yet, she still wasn't sure all of this was a good idea.

"I have to be honest with you, Miles. I want to be with you, but the Café is all-consuming right now. It's not fair for you to wait around while I try to save my business."

"Why don't you let me decide what's fair and what's not?" he said. "Because right now, the only thing that doesn't seem fair is to cut short something that has the potential to become everything."

CHAPTER NINETEEN

"And one with sprinkles." Miles tapped the pastry case. "How many is that?"

"One dozen," Levi replied as he folded the cardboard lid down on the pink box. "Can I get you guys anything else?"

"Nope, I think that'll do it." Miles passed Levi his credit card and motioned for Cooper to step back from the glass. The little boy's breath left fog on the surface, like a frozen mist on a window in the middle of winter. "Thanks, Levi. These look delicious."

"They taste delicious too. I can vouch for that." He patted his stomach in jest and handed Miles the receipt. "Hey, if you've got a minute, swing by Chloe's shop. She's been wanting to get your print to you and I told her I would relay the info if I saw you."

Miles had completely forgotten about the piece Chloe had been working on for them. Cooper had gotten sick, things with Scarlett went south, and time had gotten away from him. He felt bad about that.

"That's right. Thanks for the reminder. We'll head in that direction right now. See you around, Levi."

Miles put Cooper in charge of carrying the box of donuts. It was a risky move, but the boy had begged and begged and promised he could handle it. Shuffling along the sidewalk with his tongue thrust out in deep concentration, Cooper held the box like it was full of precious treasure.

"When can I eat one, Daddy?"

"Right after we pick up our artwork from Chloe's place."

"But my tummy is growling right now."

"Then you'll just have to tell it to wait a couple more minutes."

Cooper's lips bent into a dissatisfied frown, but he didn't press his father on it.

When they came up to *Love Letters*, Miles opened the door for Cooper to pass through first, then followed him inside the shop. Classical music played softly over the speakers and Miles noticed a small water feature that trickled near the entrance door, ushering even more calm into the already tranquil space. The place was ripe for creativity and Miles could easily see why Chloe used this as her studio, as well as her storefront.

"Miles!" Chloe looked up from her desk near the register. "I'm so glad you finally came by. I've been meaning to get this to you and just kept forgetting to get in touch." She pulled on a drawer and withdrew the print. She raised it up for Miles to see, her face aglow with expectation. "I hope you like what I did with it."

How couldn't he? It was now perfect with the addition of himself and Cooper in the foreground, complete with Orson dangling from Cooper's little hand. Miles had never seen himself as an illustration before. The caricature was something out of a children's book, and it warmed his heart more than he could express.

"Chloe, this is amazing." He took the print and looked it over more closely. "You are unbelievably talented."

"Thank you. I liked it before, but I think it really feels custom now with your likeness on it. And it goes so well with the saying, *Home is Wherever I'm with You.* I'm glad you like it."

"I love it." He reached around for his wallet. "How much do I owe?"

She flapped a hand at him. "It's on me."

"I can't accept that. You spent so long on this."

"Some things I create to sell; other things I create to gift. This falls into the second category."

The generosity in this town knew no end. "Well, I really appreciate that. Cooper and I will treasure this. And I've got the perfect spot for it in our room."

"How are things going over at the Inn?"

"Great. Our bed is really comfortable, and that's more than I can say for the one on our tour bus." Out of the corner of his eye, he saw Cooper slowly lift the lid to the pink box. "Not now, buddy. Just a few more minutes."

"I can't wait a few more minutes. My tummy is getting really loud."

"Sure you can," Miles said. "Why don't you offer Chloe one?"

"She can't have the one with the sprinkles. That one's mine."

"Cooper." Miles scolded. "That's not nice at all. We need to share."

"If those donuts came from where I think they did, I've already had two this morning," Chloe said with a wink. "And I agree, Cooper. The ones with the sprinkles are the absolute best."

Miles smiled, relieved that his son's behavior hadn't been completely off-putting. He sometimes forgot that four-year-olds didn't have filters. "Thank you again for the print, Chloe. We really do appreciate it."

"Of course. Happy to be even a small piece in making this place feel more like home."

COOPER DIDN'T MENTION THE DONUTS AGAIN WHILE they walked to the park, so Miles rewarded his son's patience with not only one sprinkled treat, but half of another chocolate glazed, which they split. He knew the sugar high would only last a short while before

Cooper came crashing down, but the park was a good place to run off that energy.

It was crowded again today, but they didn't mind. If anything, it was good for Cooper to meet other children. Especially since they'd decided to extend their stay in Harmony Ridge. Miles found a comfortable bench in the sun and pulled out his phone to scan the news on an app.

Every so often, he would look up and connect with Cooper, just to check in and make sure his son stayed close. He had found a little girl about his age and together they plopped down in the sand in the middle of the playground, shoveling scoops of dirt to construct a messy castle. The girl had fire-engine red hair that curled in spirals around her face, and the freckles that dotted her nose were downright adorable.

"Is that one yours?"

The voice lifted his attention from his phone, and Miles shaded his brow to glimpse the silhouetted figure that came into view beside him. He didn't need to be told; he was confident it was the girl's mother. That same ginger hair and smattering of freckles was a dead giveaway.

"The sugar-powered boy getting sand all over your daughter? Yep, he would be mine."

The mother lowered her eyes toward the space on the bench beside Miles, her gaze wordlessly requesting an invitation to sit.

"Would you like to join me?" He motioned next to him.

"I would," she answered, lowering down onto the bench. "But what I'd really like is one of those donuts."

"How could I be so rude?" Miles lifted the lid. "Take your pick. Although I can't promise they haven't all been handled by a four-year-old."

"I live with one too. I'm not afraid," she said with a laugh that felt only half genuine. "I think we've seen you at storytime."

"Oh, yeah? Cooper and I like to go to that. Sorry I didn't recognize you. My concentration is usually focused on keeping Cooper from wiggling right out of his seat. That kid has endless energy."

"Cooper's his name?" she asked. "My daughter's name is Ava." She held Miles' gaze for a moment. "And I'm Carly."

"Nice to meet you." He shook her hand, then reciprocated the introduction. "Miles."

"Hi, Miles." She was a beautiful woman with a warmness about her Miles liked. "I promise this isn't a pickup line, but are you new here?"

"We are. Newish, at least."

"Did you move into that new subdivision off Lincoln? I've been meeting a lot of new families from that area lately. Beautiful homes."

"No, we're actually staying at the Inn. Not sure how long we'll be in town."

Her eyebrows lifted. "Oh. The Inn is a lovely place to stay. I was married there, actually."

Something about the information made Miles' shoulders slacken. He was new to the game of flirting and maybe he'd read what he assumed were Carly's advances all wrong. She was just being friendly. That was a welcome relief.

"I would think a wedding there would be beautiful. Those gardens are straight out of a magazine."

"It was beautiful. The wedding of the century, some even said." She released another stilted laugh. "I think that was the entire issue. We focused so much on the actual wedding day that we didn't put any energy into the days or months that followed," she divulged. "The wedding was beautiful. The marriage...not so much."

That was a lot of information between strangers, and Miles wasn't sure what to do with it. "I'm sorry to hear that."

"All's well that ends well, right?" She shrugged a little and bit into a donut glazed with pink icing. Her fingers moved to her lips to brush off a stray crumb. "Looks like our kids get along nicely."

Miles moved his focus toward the two children playing in the sand, taking turns with the shovels and buckets. "Looks like."

"We should plan a date."

His neck snapped, head swiveling Carly's direction. "What?"

"We should plan a playdate for them." She lifted

her chin toward the sandbox. "Ava would love to have the company. I don't know about Cooper, but she gets lonely as an only child." Reaching into her large designer purse, Carly pulled out a piece of scrap paper and a pen. She clicked the retractable end and scribbled something before passing off the paper to Miles. "That's my number. Give me a call or text and we can set something up."

Carly had gone out of her way earlier in their conversation to say she wasn't picking him up, but Miles couldn't ignore the inkling that she was shamelessly flirting with him. Still, Cooper needed friends his own age. It was good to see him having fun. And a simple playdate was likely innocent enough. Wasn't it?

"I need to chat with one of the moms over there about a multi-level marketing party she invited me to. Is there a polite way to say 'I'm not interested in your pyramid scheme' other than just coming out with it?"

"I can't say I've ever had to decline an invitation to something like that."

"Oh, give it time. You hang around this park long enough and all the moms will invite you to something." She fluttered a less-than-innocent wink in his direction as she rose to her feet. "Glad I could be the first."

CHAPTER TWENTY

"*N*ora Paisley is out front." Dominic didn't look up as he flicked his wrist to flip the perfectly browned grilled cheese on the sizzling pan. "I set her up in a corner booth with a coffee on the house. Told her you'd be able to meet with her in a few."

"Nora?" Scarlett searched her brain, but came up empty.

"The beekeeper. Young gal who came by here earlier this spring to see about offering her honey in our Café? Ring a bell?"

Revelation slammed into Scarlett with the force of a freight truck. "Oh, my goodness! I completely blanked on that! I told her to come back when her hives were producing, didn't I?"

"Yep. Sure did." Dominic smiled. "And it sounds like they finally are."

Scarlett's stomach turned in on itself. She vaguely

remembered the woman, but she did recall both liking her and promising to support her in this new endeavor. But that was back when resources weren't so strapped and funds were more readily available. She couldn't see how she could possibly be any help to her now. "I'll see what I can work out with her. Thank you, Dom."

He slid the sandwich onto a plate, grabbed a handful of crispy, homemade potato chips from the bin nearby, and passed off the lunch to Timmy before starting in on the next order.

The restaurant was quieter today. That shouldn't really come as a relief because of their current financial situation, but Scarlett sank into the stillness of it all. It gave her brain the extra room it needed to sort things through, starting with the situation with the beekeeper.

She found the woman seated in the corner booth, an array of glass jars displayed on the table in front of her, that golden, rich liquid filling each container to the brim. Little gingham ribbons secured tags to the bottles and as Scarlett stepped closer, she could make out the branding: Sweet Harmony Honey.

Oh goodness, she loved everything about it.

"Nora!" She held her arms out in welcome as the young woman rose from her seat for a hug. "I'm so sorry to keep you waiting. I hope it hasn't been long."

"I'm very patient," Nora supplied with a smile. "After all, my little coworkers have trained me to be. Everything happens on their timetable." She slipped back into the booth. Scarlett joined her. "As promised, I'm back with my harvest. These last few months, I've spent a lot of time researching how a partnership with your Café could greatly benefit both parties. I think you'll like what I've come up with."

She made a move for a leather-bound notebook, but Scarlett stopped her.

"Nora, things have changed since the last time we talked."

The woman's face fell. "Oh…"

"I would still love to use your product in our store. I just don't think I'll be able to fulfill the numbers we originally discussed."

"That's totally fine," Nora said, but Scarlett could easily see the enthusiasm slip right out from her, like a balloon quickly deflated. "I'm not looking for a huge account, Scarlett. Just a place to serve my product and get my foot in the door, so to speak."

"I would love to be able to provide that for you, but the Café…" Scarlett could scarcely catch her breath to continue the sentence. "It's fallen on hard times."

"Oh no. I'm very sorry to hear that."

"We've actually started sourcing some of our ingredients from Hamilton." It came out with all the insult of a dirty word. "I hate to even admit that out loud. You know I love to support local, and I'm especially passionate about working with other female entrepreneurs."

"I totally get it, Scarlett. You need to do what's

best for your business. If you already have an account for your honey products with a company in Hamilton, that's completely understandable."

Scarlett could sense her convictions slowly slip through her grasp, like sand filtering through her fingers. Supporting local businesses. Offering quality, ethically sourced products. And most importantly, keeping her word. She'd given Nora hope months back when they'd talked, and now here she was, going back on that. It wasn't something she could do.

"How about you leave a couple of jars and I'll talk to my chef and see what he thinks about incorporating them into some dishes? And even if we aren't able to give you as much business as we'd originally committed to, I'm more than happy to offer a space in our Café where you can display and sell your products. We can work out a consignment type of arrangement, if you're comfortable with that."

"That would be amazing!" Nora's entire countenance perked up. "Honestly, I'm just trying to get my name and product out there. Any way you can help with that works for me."

"Thank you for being so understanding, Nora. I wish I could give you more of a commitment, but we're doing everything we can to stay afloat right now and bringing on new accounts just isn't the best business move."

"No apologies necessary." Nora began to pack up her display. "I really hope you're able to turn things around, regardless of whether or not my products are in your Café. This place has always been such a staple in our community. I couldn't imagine anything ever changing that."

"THIS IS EXACTLY WHAT I NEEDED, EUGENE." Scarlett's lips touched the mouth of the glass bottle. "Thank you for inviting me over."

She pressed her ballet flats to the porch deck and rocked the chair back. The cool drink had done its work to loosen her muscles and mind, and for that, she was grateful. Plus, Eugene was always good company. Sometimes she wondered if she looked to him as a father figure—someone to fill in the role the absence of her own father created. Put simply, Eugene was a friend. And a good one. Not every relationship needed a strict label.

That was a startling thought that took Scarlett by the collar and shook her.

Maybe that was where things had gone wrong with Miles, this need to label things. Her feelings were just that—feelings. They didn't have to be explained, and they certainly didn't need to be defined. That was a freedom, and when she allowed herself to think of things that way, it didn't feel so constricting.

"Lottie told me she loved me today."

Scarlett stopped drinking mid-swallow and looked across the porch. "Eugene! Congratulations! That's huge."

His face didn't match the joy she expected to accompany the announcement.

"I couldn't say it back," he admitted quietly.

"That's okay, Eugene. I'm certain her declaration wasn't based on receiving one in return. She probably just wanted you to know how she felt."

He took a long pull from the bottle in his hands, then settled the drink in his lap. "She might not have expected it, but I figure she at least hoped for it." He rocked so slowly the chair hardly moved. "I haven't said those words to anyone since Doris."

"Oh, Eugene. I can imagine that's very difficult."

"When I told Doris I loved her, it was like that phrase was only meant for her. Like she owned those three little words. Just like she owned my heart."

"Do you love Lottie?"

"Sure, I do."

"Do you love her the same way you loved Doris?"

His bushy eyebrows bunched together. "'Course not. It's still love, but it's different."

"You can say the same phrase to two different people, but have a different meaning behind it."

"Not sure I'll ever be ready to say those words again," he spoke softly in a voice that quaked with emotion.

"That's okay too. Maybe there's a different way you can tell her how you feel. Or show her."

"You think so?"

"Absolutely, I do. The expression of love is limitless."

He lifted his drink and took another long pull, then rested it on the metal table between them. His hands folded together, thumbs twirling round and round the other. "That something you think you can help me do? Show Lottie I love her?"

It fell drastically outside of Scarlett's wheelhouse. She'd never been in love. But helping her friends was right up her alley, and she had plenty of experience in that area.

"Of course I can help. For starters, let's think of all the things you love about her."

In record time, they made a list on a notepad they'd gotten from the Inn's kitchen, including everything from Lottie's patience when Eugene told long-winded stories to her snazzy pink shoes she wore with nearly every outfit. He especially liked those. Listening to Eugene detail his affection for his sweetheart was heartwarming. With every little thing he noted, that spark in his eye seemed to intensify.

He was completely smitten with the woman.

"Eugene, this is quite a comprehensive list." Scarlett scanned it over. "You could just give this to her. Then she'd know exactly how you feel."

"I can't do that." His head whipped side to side. "She'd think it's silly."

"I don't think so. Women tend to appreciate compliments, and we've written down so many here. I think she'd be incredibly flattered."

"All those words…" He waved his hand toward

the scrap piece of paper. "They still don't add up to the three she said to me."

"I think they do, Eugene. Maybe even more so." Scarlett flipped the cover back around on the spiral notepad. "You know what? Let's table this for now. There's no rush. What do you say we go down to the Café and grab a milkshake? My treat."

"Can't." He rolled his wrist to look at his watch. "I'm picking Lottie up to take her to her doctor's appointment soon. She's waiting to hear some results on a scan she had last week. Insisted I don't need to go, but I can't imagine her sitting in that waiting room all by herself. Told her I'd be there for her, no matter what."

"You know, Eugene, that gesture right there is your version of those three little words." Scarlett's hand came down on her friend's shoulder. "But I'm pretty sure she already knows it."

CHAPTER TWENTY-ONE

"Got your cape, buddy?" Miles unzipped Cooper's backpack to make sure everything he would need was still inside. They'd packed it up the night before, but things had a way of disappearing with a four-year-old around.

"Oops! I forgot." Cooper flung open the accordion door of their closet and stretched up on his toes to yank the apron from a wire hanger. "Here it is."

"Perfect. And you'll be on your best behavior for Levi?"

"Yes, Daddy," Cooper huffed, annoyed that the question even had to be asked. "Promise."

Levi reiterated on multiple occasions that he was more than happy to have Cooper hang out at the bakery for a few hours here and there, but Miles wasn't one to take advantage of that generosity. Until he made more connections in Harmony Ridge, he'd have to rely on the limited number of people he did trust. Luckily, those precious few never made Cooper feel like a nuisance or a bother. Quite the opposite.

Today, when Miles dropped Cooper off, Levi said that rather than baking, they'd be doing a little construction project. Miles wasn't sure what that entailed, but it didn't matter. Levi always made it a good time for his son. Today would likely be no different.

This afternoon, Miles' drive to the high school campus was more easily made, the roads and parking lot nearly empty, allowing him to get there in record time. School had gotten out for the summer just the week before and there was an almost eerie quiet as he crossed the campus toward the administration building. His feet met the pavement too loudly, echoing in the empty halls and pinging off the walls like a game of pinball.

He reached for his bowtie and tugged. It felt tight and pressed against his Adam's apple, much too constricting and altogether uncomfortable. But this was the appropriate attire for an interview, he assumed. He wanted to present himself in the best possible way, and a piece of that was looking the part.

Still, you could dress up all you wanted and that wouldn't take the place of experience. When it came to teaching, he had none. He was a talented musician, but that didn't qualify him for the position. He could make a lengthy list of guitarists whose skills were unparalleled. Second to none, even. But put them in a classroom with a bunch of high school kids? They would flounder and fail. Just because someone excelled in something didn't mean they could teach it to others. Being gifted didn't always make one qualified.

That mantra floated in and out of his brain, slipping back into his thoughts as he tried and failed to give himself a pep talk.

"What are you even doing here, Callahan?" he muttered under his breath as he took the handle to the office door within his grasp and opened it wide.

A teenage girl sat behind the front desk, head bopping to whatever music played in her large teal headphones. She chewed on the eraser end of her pencil and all but threw the writing implement across the room when she noticed Miles standing above her.

"You scared me!" she shouted, shoulders heaving with an erratic breath. Suddenly, her gaze tightened. She scanned Miles up and down. "You're…" Pulling the wires looped around her neck, the headphones popped free. "You're from Timber Rose!"

"Miles Callahan," he confirmed.

The teenager just stared, mouth agape. Miles could glimpse a pink wad of gum smashed against her molars.

"I have a meeting with Principal Darcy." He peered over the ledge of the desk toward the appointment book placed in front of the girl. He perused for his name, then tapped on it with his index finger. "Right here. That's me. Two o'clock."

"I cannot believe I'm sitting here listening to

Timber Rose's newest single and in walks the lead guitar player from that very band!" She picked up her phone and immediately started tapping something out on it, punching wildly across the screen. "Wait until my friends hear about this!"

Miles' brain tripped over her sentence. "Newest single?"

"Yeah, the one that dropped on MusicHub this morning. It's so good. You guys are crazy talented." Her palms slammed down onto the desk. "Oh, my gosh! Are you going to work here? Is Lana with you?"

"No...no, she's not." Miles' head twitched. "You said newest single..."

"You don't believe me, do you?" The student thrust out the set of headphones, smacking him in the chest with them. "I'm serious. I was *literally* listening to it when you walked in. Am I on some sort of hidden camera show?"

He took the headphones and placed them on just as the girl hit the play icon on her phone.

Miles' knees buckled.

"What is this?" he asked, but he didn't need to. He knew every note of the song. He'd written it, after all, and he'd played it for Cooper whenever he requested it. For goodness' sake, he even played it to a dog just last week.

How was this even possible?

Pulling them from his ears, Miles passed the headphones back, shock slowing his movements like he'd been drowned in molasses.

"Can I get a selfie?" the girl blurted, not even waiting for a reply before she was up and around the desk, clicking away on her camera while Mile stood there, utterly dumbfounded and expressionless.

"Ah, Mr. Callahan." At that same moment, the door to Principal Darcy's office swung open and Miles had to do a double-take before his brain could register things correctly. Carly from the park smiled widely at him, her countenance friendly and familiar. "I thought I heard you out here. I'm glad you could make it."

Squeezing his eyes briefly shut, Miles drew in a sharp breath, smoothed his hand down his button-up shirt, and paced toward the woman. Curve balls hurled at him from every direction, but he needed to pull himself together. "Nice to see you again, Principal Darcy."

"The pleasure's all mine. Please, come in." Carly wore a fitted gray pantsuit and had her hair done up in a twist, pinned with a silver clip at the crown of her head. She straddled the line between professional and intimidating, and suddenly Miles was entirely out of his element. Conversation had been easy the other day at the park when they talked about their common woes as parents of young children. But a job interview was a completely different animal. Other than his first job flipping burgers in high school, he'd never been interviewed, and that insecurity coursed through him, colliding with the shock he still hadn't processed regarding the song.

He was a certifiable mess, and his gut rumbled with the nausea overtaking him.

Evidently, he looked as bad as he felt.

"Can I get you a glass of water, Mr. Callahan?"

Miles fiddled with his bowtie. It had an all-out chokehold on him now. "Yes, that would be great." He coughed. "Thank you."

Principal Darcy retreated to the back of the office near the water cooler. The jug bubbled loudly as she filled a cup from the spout, the sound unsettling, making Miles' stomach churn all the more.

"I'm sorry," he said. "Is there a restroom nearby?"

"There is. Right outside this office and down the hall on your left."

He half-stood. "Would you excuse me for a moment?"

"Certainly. Please feel free to let yourself back in. No need to knock." She motioned for the door with a nod and a fluttering hand. "I'll be right here."

Miles rushed toward the men's room. With his back slumped against the cold, hard surface, he shut the door at the same moment his knees unhinged. Like a sack of potatoes, he dropped to the tiled floor, collapsing into a position that no grown man would expect to find himself in.

Curled in a heap, he took out his phone and typed.

Lana, we need to talk.

Funny, Lana had been trying to get ahold of him earlier and he'd ignored her many attempts. Was this what she'd wanted to discuss with him? He should have just taken her calls, but the entire point of setting out on the road was to place some distance between them. He didn't want to be at Lana's beck and call anymore, and he'd been stubborn about that. Maybe a little too stubborn.

Now it felt as though everything was imploding and he wondered if that one decision to ignore her had set it all in motion.

The phone buzzed, making his heart stutter into high gear like he'd been shocked with a defibrillator.

I take it you heard it.

The acidic tinge of bile came up his throat. His vision blurred and his fingers locked as he attempted to punch out a reply.

That song belongs to me, Lana. Not the band.

Dots trailed across the screen as she typed, an anxiety-inducing ellipses.

Well, I believe you took off with something —or should I say, someONE—that belongs to me. And that's a whole lot more important than a silly song.

What on Earth did she mean by that?

A knock on the other side of the door snapped Miles to attention.

"Everything okay in there, Mr. Callahan?" Principal Darcy inquired warily.

Humiliation caused sweat to bead on Miles' brow.

"Yep. Just fine." He jumped to his feet. "Just think I ate some bad tuna fish for lunch. I'll be right out."

I can't do this with you right now, Lana. But whatever you did needs to be undone.

He didn't wait for a reply, just shoved the phone into his pocket and headed back into the interview.

Lana had ruined a lot for him over the years. He wasn't about to let her ruin the one thing that could guarantee him a future in Harmony Ridge.

CHAPTER TWENTY-TWO

*S*carlett bowed out of her work day early that Thursday afternoon and she didn't let herself feel any guilt over it.

She was going to create some margin in her life. That was the plan. It wasn't a solid one yet, since she'd stayed at the Café until ten the night before, washing dishes and crunching numbers. That couldn't really be considered cutting back. But today was a new day and determination filled her like a breath of fresh mountain air.

The farmers' market was in full swing, vibrant and alive with mouthwatering aromas and pulsing music, an absolute feast for the senses. The ambiance was perfect. Summer had settled into the valley with all the restful promise of slower days and longer nights. Scarlett loved this time of year. Students were out of school and into the Café more, and they brought with them an energy the typical clientele didn't possess.

And, oddly enough, they brought in dollars. Lots of them. Scarlett couldn't make any sense of it. How was it possible that high school students gladly paid their full tab when the older, working customers often skipped out? It was a puzzle she couldn't solve, but nothing needed to be done about it at the present moment. Tonight was about savoring her surroundings and the experience, and she had every intention of doing just that.

She spent longer than she needed at the jellies and jams booth, sampling from both the peach jalapeño and strawberry basil preserves with little, disposable wooden spoons. The combination of ingredients was delightful, and her taste buds danced with each new flavor. She bought three jars—two for herself and one as a gift for her mother—and then moved onto the next booth.

Tony Huppert stood behind a folding table adorned with a red and white checkered tablecloth. Crusty breads and fresh loaves sat on display in baskets and were tucked into wooden crates, creating a makeshift bakery in the middle of the market.

"Nice to see you out here, Scarlett," Tony said as he ran his serrated knife through an Asiago loaf. The bread crunched beneath the blade. "You need to try this one. It's our current best seller."

Scarlett could easily see why. Sharp, pungent cheeses melted over the top of the soft, doughy bread and it made for a delectable mix. "Oh goodness, that's delicious. I'll take one of those." She pointed to another smaller bread loaf, this one baked and molded into the shape of a robot, complete with two raisins for eyes. "And that one too. I have someone in mind who will just love it."

"I sure do have a lot of fun making these." Tony smiled as he wrapped up the baked goods and read Scarlett her total. "How are things at the Café?"

"Oh, you know how the food industry is. We have our ups and downs." She slipped the loaves into her canvas tote bag and offered a smile, but had to work at making it truly genuine.

"That I do. I hope it's more up than down for you from here on out."

"Thank you, Tony. I appreciate it. Take care."

They waved their goodbyes, and Scarlett worked her way down the first row of vendors.

It stayed light much later into the evening this time of year, and she savored the long, drawn out day for all it was worth. The temperature was balmy, her cheery, yellow sundress was the perfect attire, and her mood felt light as a soap bubble. Not much could make the evening more enjoyable.

Then she saw them. In the distance, just a few yards up, were Miles and Cooper, hand in hand, arms swinging joyfully between them. Her heart hiccupped at the sight, then picked up tempo when Miles' gaze anchored onto hers from across the market.

Those cerulean eyes captivated her the way seeing the deep blue of the ocean for the first time made you lose your breath. He held the connection as they made their way through the crowd toward her, and when he came up to her, a slow smile growing on his lips and hope in his eyes, she wanted to throw her arms around his neck and hug him.

But they'd taken a step back and a greeting like that didn't feel appropriate. Especially when she'd been the one to request a little space.

"I didn't think I'd find you here tonight," Miles said. "What a pleasant surprise." He moved close and left a kiss on her cheek. Suddenly she wished she would have just gone in for the hug too.

"It is," she agreed. She bent down to Cooper's level. "You know, it's serendipity that you're here."

"That weird word again." Cooper made a face.

Scarlett chuckled. "I have something for you." She withdrew the robot bread loaf and passed it to the boy. "Something about it made me think of you. I remember you really liked that cartoon with all those junkyard robots."

Miles laughed, though it sounded a bit like a snort. "We actually have something for you too." He had a similar canvas tote slung over his shoulder, the words Harmony Ridge Market screen printed across the fabric. Dipping his hand into the bag, he pulled out a matching loaf, but this one was shaped into the likeness of a bear. "Cooper thought it would remind you of our bear hunt."

"I just love it! It's perfect, Cooper. Thank you so much." She pushed back up and looked directly at Miles. "How have you been?"

"I've been hanging in there," he admitted. "I've been meaning to call—"

"It's okay, Miles. I know we're both busy."

"We are, but I'm never too busy for you, Scarlett. I hope you know that."

She was going to have to pull her gaze away if he kept looking at her like that—like she was the only person in the entire market. There was a weightlessness to her stomach that only Miles seemed to elicit. And try as she might to ignore it, she just couldn't. She was attracted to him in every possible way, from his undeniably handsome looks to his tender heart to the way he parented his precious son.

And yet, she'd asked to take a step back. The very real possibility that she could lose this incredible man and whatever this was between them loomed over her like a cloud, heavy and hazy with the threat of rain.

Scarlett sucked in a breath. "Hey, any chance you two are hungry? I was just about to grab a gyro from the food truck and set up a little picnic for myself over at the tables across the lawn. I'd love for you to join me if you haven't already eaten."

The word picnic brought with it specific memories of the night of their first kiss, and that hollow feeling dipped through her stomach again.

"What do you say, Coop?" Miles shifted his attention down to his son. "You feel like some Greek food?"

"Yup," the boy agreed, and they all moved toward the food truck and filtered into line.

Miles insisted on paying and Scarlett let him. After their order was prepared and their number called, the three started off slowly across the sprawling green grass. Cooper suddenly erupted into a sprint when he caught sight of a flock of ducks near the pond's edge. Birds quacked raucously and fluttered into flight when the boy came barreling in with arms flailed and a voice full of high-pitched delight.

"Careful, buddy! Slow up before you get to that water," Miles shouted over the expanse of rolling lawn between them. He kept his eyes trained on Cooper until the boy's feet skidded to a stop a safe distance from the water. He returned his attention to Scarlett. "I don't want to overstep, but do you mind me asking how things are going at the Café?"

"You know? They're actually going pretty good. School's out, so we've got more kids coming through, which has surprisingly been better for business. I'm more hopeful today than I was last week, so I guess that's a good thing."

"Hope is always a good thing." Miles hiked his leg to straddle the bench, then lowered himself to the seat and their food to the table. "I've been wanting to share something with you, Scarlett, but I haven't figured out how to."

She'd joined him along the same side of the picnic table and had just unwrapped her piping hot lamb gyro to take a bite, but his words made her pause. "Is everything okay?"

"I think it is. I'm just hoping you will too."

He was scaring her with this deliberate hesitation. "Just tell me, Miles. Please."

"I applied for that music teacher job at the high school and got it."

"Miles! That's great news."

"Is it?" His forehead tensed, eyes tightening at the corners. "I know you wanted to slow things down between us, mostly because you weren't sure about my timeline for hanging around Harmony Ridge. And I don't want you to think I applied for the job just so things could work out between us. I mean, of course you were a factor. But I mainly just want stability for Cooper. And this one-year commitment will give him that."

It was all the news she had ever hoped to hear— that Miles and Cooper would remain in town—and yet the overwhelm of excitement didn't rush through her. And that had a little to do with Miles' stagnant expression.

"What aren't you telling me?"

His throat worked on a swallow. "Lana—my ex— is up to something."

"That's kind of vague."

"It's vague only because it's all I know right now. She's pulled a little stunt that I'd rather not discuss at the moment, but I'm worried she's going to make life more challenging for me for the unforeseeable future."

Scarlett's hand covered Miles'. "Don't let her steal

your joy, Miles. You have every right to celebrate this new job and this new beginning."

"Well, she's already stolen one of my songs, and she's threatening to steal much, much more." He lifted his shoulders and inhaled. "But enough about that. I agree—getting that teaching job was a win I wasn't counting on, and that deserves to be celebrated." He raised his soda can and clinked it to Scarlett's. "To new beginnings."

"To new beginnings," she echoed and took a sip of the fizzy liquid, unable to shake the thought that all beginnings had endings, and praying whatever Lana had up her sleeve wouldn't hasten theirs.

CHAPTER TWENTY-THREE

*J*ust after eight the next morning, the shrill tone of the bedside phone ringing next to his ear rattled Miles out of a restful slumber.

Yesterday had been pulled straight out of a dream. Miles even briefly wondered if it all had been one. The job offer for the high school position that he was admittedly under qualified for. Running into Scarlett at the market and sharing a picnic dinner and hope-filled conversation about their respective futures, neither quite ready to broach the topic of a shared future, but knowing it was now within the realm of possibility. That slow yet solid embrace she gave him as they parted ways at the end of their night, lingering in the parking lot long after everyone else had packed up and closed down.

But even as so much of his day was undeniably dreamlike, there were equal parts containing all the trappings of a veritable nightmare. Fear. Uncertainty. Lana's cryptic threats. That was life, he supposed. The good and the bad. Yin and Yang.

In reality, Lana was the reason for the sense of dread that quickened his heart rate when the phone trilled a second time. Avoidance wasn't a permanent solution. Eventually, she would come looking for answers. Looking for him. Miles knew better than to think he could outrun a woman scorned, even if she was in the wrong on practically all accounts.

Fumbling for the receiver, his hand collided with the phone just as it rang a third time. He pulled it free and lifted it to his ear, keeping his voice low so as not to wake Cooper resting beside him in the bed.

"Hello?" He expelled the word in a whisper.

"Good morning, Mr. Callahan. It's Beth, the innkeeper. So sorry to wake you."

He knew he couldn't mask the grogginess in his tone, but he still said, "Oh, you didn't wake me, Beth. I've been up for a bit. Is everything okay?"

The thick pause on the line provided his answer before her words confirmed them. "Well, I think so. I'm not really sure. I'm calling because there's a woman down here." Beth's volume lowered to an almost imperceptible hush. "She's actually asleep on the loveseat in the drawing room. *Sound* asleep. I can't seem to wake her, and I've purposefully been banging things around in the kitchen all morning just to see if I could rouse her. I've done all I can at this point."

"Sounds like you need some help getting this

woman up and sending her on her way. I can be down in less than five minutes. Just let me throw on some clothes. Hang tight."

"Miles…I think she's probably here to see you."

Miles jolted upright. His spine pressed against the headboard, instantly drawn to attention.

"What would make you think that?"

"The Timber Rose sticker on her suitcase."

Stifling his groan was as easy as swallowing a bucket of thumbtacks.

There were several straightforward explanations. A groupie who discovered his whereabouts and thought it would be fun to crash his stay at the Inn. Nothing like that had ever happened to him before, but it wasn't outside the realm of possibility. Lana had adoring admirers tracking down her location all the time. She even once had an overzealous fan that took things a little too far. Showing up at her house. Waiting outside her doctor's office. Frequenting her favorite restaurants and coffeehouses. It wasn't unheard of for a fan to cross the line into stalker territory, but it didn't feel plausible in this instance. Miles wasn't the truly famous one in the band.

Every scenario Miles manufactured involving a fan felt less and less likely.

The only woman so desperate to find him she would sleep on an old piece of furniture in a strange new town was Lana.

Unease tumbled through his gut.

"I'll be right down, Beth. Thanks for the heads up."

He rolled over and reached across the bed to tuck the comforter up under Cooper's chin. His son looked so angelic as he slumbered, so full of innocence and promise. Miles wanted the best for him. He wanted to protect him and provide for him and create a life they both loved.

For years, he wanted Lana to be a part of that. There wasn't anything romantic about it. He didn't love her, didn't want to be united as husband and wife as any sort of declaration of adoration. No, he just wanted Cooper to have both a mom and a dad. Stability. That was the simple, unadulterated truth of it all.

As Miles scrubbed a toothbrush across his teeth, he wondered if maybe Lana had finally realized a life with her son was better than a life without one. This wasn't wishful thinking anymore. Miles no longer made, nor even held onto, that wish. In fact, the recent distance between them just proved how good it felt to remove that toxicity clear out of his life. To remove Lana as a whole.

He cranked the faucet and splashed frigid water over his face, then blotted it dry with a towel, preparing himself with a big, intentional breath that left fog on the mirror. Dressing in record time, he checked in on Cooper once more before bounding out of the room and down the creaking staircase two at a time.

Beth wasn't joking; Miles could hear the innkeeper clanking and clinking away in the kitchen, pots and pans crashing together in a jarring cacophony of cookware noise. It was enough to wake and rattle the bones of the dead.

Steeling himself for everything an unwanted encounter with Lana involved, he inhaled to full capacity again and rounded the corner into the front room.

Just like Beth had noted on the phone call, there was the figure of a woman, all curled up and seemingly quite comfortable on the small loveseat under the bay window overlooking Harmony Lane. Her position left her with her back to him, and the hoodie lifted up and over her head disguised her identity completely.

Moving forward with quiet steps, Miles tiptoed further into the room. He cleared his throat once.

She didn't even stir.

One more time and still nothing.

"Lana?" His vocal cords constricted as the name escaped his lips. "Lana, is that you?"

The form rustled.

"Hey, it's time to wake up now." Miles' hand found her shoulder and jostled a little. Then, with all the force of sudden awareness, the woman flipped around. Her wild eyes locked in on Miles.

"Maddie?" He nearly screamed it. "Maddie? What are you doing here?"

His sister balled a fist and jammed it into one eye

socket, then the other, rubbing vigorously like windshield washers blinking back a torrential storm. "Oh good! I *am* in the right place," she exclaimed with unmistakable relief. "It was so dark when I got in last night that I wasn't sure the driver had dropped me off at the right spot. This town doesn't have a lot of streetlights. Did you know that?"

Maddie righted her position on the antique sofa, rolled out her shoulders in big, dramatic circles, then wobbled her head to crack her neck.

"Maddie, what are you doing here? I had no idea you were coming."

"Because I didn't tell you."

"And why didn't you tell me?"

She yawned loudly. "Because you would have told me not to come."

She was probably right about that, but knowing *why* she wanted to come could have changed that. "Seriously, Maddie. What are you doing here?"

"I heard what Lana did, Miles." Familiar eyes met his. "With your song. *Cooper's* song. It's a stupid publicity stunt to get your attention. But I'm sure you already know that."

"I figured as much." He rubbed the back of his neck, then took a seat in the high-back chair across from his sister. Leaning forward, elbows digging into his knees, and hands clasped below his chin, he blinked her into focus, praying she would stay there. Whatever the reason for her arrival, it was sure good to be with her. "All of that still doesn't explain why you're here. A simple text could've relayed that information. You didn't have to pack up and come all the way out to Harmony Ridge."

Something resembling sympathy locked in on her face, and Maddie's gaze shifted before she peered around Miles and into the kitchen behind him. "Is there somewhere private we can talk? Somewhere out of earshot?"

"I have a room upstairs. But Cooper is still sleeping."

She nodded. "You know what? For now, let's just enjoy the fact that you and I are in the same zip code again. I say that calls for a breakfast celebration."

"We can do breakfast. Sure. There's a great little café I'd love to take you to. But you're not off the hook about telling me why you're really here. You need to know that. This isn't a pass."

"I know I'm not. And I'll fill you in on everything, I promise. But all they served me on the plane last night was a dinky bag of pretzels. I'm famished. Things will be a lot better once I get some food in my belly and some snuggles from my favorite nephew in my arms."

"I can't believe you're really here, Mads." Miles' head swayed side to side, awed by the fact that after weeks apart, they were finally in the same room again. Family never felt so good. "It's so nice to see you face to face. Cooper's going to be thrilled."

"He better be! I've missed my little Cooper Trooper more than words can even say. Hey, what do you say we go wake him up?" She jumped from the couch and grabbed the handle of her luggage. Only now did that Timber Rose sticker make Miles smile and not cringe over the thought of it on someone else's suitcase. "Can I do the honors?"

Waking a slumbering child was at the top of the universal list of parenting no-no's, but this surprise was too good to contain. Cooper would be over the moon to see his aunt again.

"Absolutely. He's going to think he's dreaming."

———

If Maddie had been a kangaroo, Cooper would've climbed into her pouch and stayed there forever. The boy couldn't get enough of his aunt and he absorbed all of her affection like a little thirsty sponge.

As predicted, Cooper awoke with all the delight of a child on Christmas morning when Maddie knelt quietly by his bedside, stroking his mop of curls until his sleepy eyes peeked open, one then the other. Had anyone else still been asleep at the Inn, Cooper's squeal would've served as their shrill and sudden wakeup call.

Maddie helped her nephew get dressed in his favorite Spiderman tee and khaki shorts with large Velcro pockets for all of his treasures, and then the three decided to take the extra time to walk to Harmony Ridge Row rather than drive. It was a mild, early summer morning that shouldn't be wasted within the confines of a vehicle. On that, they all agreed.

Maddie and Cooper strode leisurely along the sidewalk, hand in hand, with Miles trucking closely behind.

"This is the park I play at." The young boy acted the role of town tour guide for his aunt. "The slide is really, really big and feels kinda scary the first time you go on it, but you get used to it. I can take you on it later. It's probably not too scary for you."

"I would love that," Maddie said. "And I'm sure it'll be less scary for me if you show me how it's done first."

"I can do that." Cooper nodded confidently. "Oh! Down that long street is where the doggies are. We read to them. Sometimes we sing to them too."

Maddie swung her gaze back toward her brother, brow lifted like an unspoken question mark.

"It's a shelter." Miles jammed his hands in his pockets. "On Tuesdays, volunteers read to the animals there. Sort of like storytime for dogs. We've gone a couple of times."

"Yup," Cooper confirmed. "We do that with Miss Scarlett."

On swivel, Maddie's head angled back again, and this time her expression was even more punctuated.

Okay, so Miles hadn't really told his sister about Scarlett. It wasn't some big secret, but he knew if he ended up making Harmony Ridge a home—even a temporary one—the thought of a relationship tying him to the town was something his sister wouldn't like. He left Nashville for that exact reason; to distance himself from a woman. Maddie would want to be certain it wasn't a woman keeping him in Harmony Ridge, and he wasn't sure that was an answer he could honestly give. It felt easier to leave that part out of the equation—and conversation—entirely.

"Miss Scarlett, huh?" She likely knew she wouldn't get the answer she wanted out of her brother, so Maddie redirected her attention to Cooper. "Is she a friend?"

"Yup. You will like her. She has binoculars with special powers. She's really good at bear hunting."

"She sounds like a very interesting lady. When do I get to meet her?"

"In about five minutes." Miles edged into their conversation. "She owns the café we're going to. And before you start thinking anything, we're not a thing."

"They just sometimes kiss," Cooper said in passing before releasing his aunt's hand to collect a shiny rock at his feet.

Maddie's head spun so quickly this time, she nearly pirouetted completely around. "Miles, I'm feeling very out of the loop here. When you told me about the job at the high school and said that you'd be staying in Harmony Ridge, you failed to mention this woman with magical binoculars who hunts bears that you sometimes kiss."

"I don't kiss bears, Maddie. That's just

ridiculous."

She slugged his shoulder. "You know what I mean."

"Do I, though? Your semantics are a little confusing," he teased, hoping to worm his way out of the conversation Maddie really wanted to have. "Let's just get some food in our stomachs before we dive into all of this: the real reason why you're here and *one* of the reasons I'm still here."

"Fine." She said the word, but wasn't satisfied. "But I expect one-hundred percent honesty."

"And I'll give that to you. I always do."

"You have to tell the truth, Daddy." Cooper rolled the rock between his fingers before tugging on the pocket flap on his shorts to stow the item away for safekeeping. "Liars' pants catch on fire."

"We can't have any pant fires," Maddie said in all seriousness. "I don't have my fire extinguisher handy."

"I'm not lying to you about anything, sis."

Maddie's lips pressed into a line, disapproval written all over her face. "You're omitting a lot, which is sort of the same."

"Breakfast," he reiterated. "Then we will each come clean. Deal?"

"Deal."

Cooper looked up at them. "You have to pinky promise. That's the only way it'll work. That's what Ava says."

Maddie lifted her finger first, then hooked it onto her brother's. "Pinky promise."

CHAPTER TWENTY-FOUR

*T*he honey display was the sweetest thing and it wasn't even the ingredients in the jars that made it so. Nora, the beekeeper, had been by the day before and Scarlett showed her to the shelving unit along the far wall where she hoped to display the consigned products. It had previously housed straws and napkins and coffee cup sleeves, but there was plenty of room on the long counter to move those items over and free up the bookcase for a different purpose.

For Scarlett, this small change was a heel to the ground, pivoting in direction, even if only slightly. Other than new cooks and wait staff—along with a handful of seasonal recipes that rotated on and off the menu—the Campfire Café remained an exact replica of the one her father had maintained all of those nostalgic years. Scarlett felt him in the very bones of the establishment. In the red pleather booths that he'd had reupholstered when the original 1960's fabric had worn down to its last fibers. In the Formica countertop that she could still see him standing behind, sweeping his white and blue checkered dish-towel across mindlessly as he chatted it up with an old friend opposite the bar. In the sharp ding of the register and rumble and slam of the cash drawer. Every inch of the Café had Jack Harmony's stamp on it. He was branded into the very atmosphere.

But this new section, however small, was all Scarlett. A mix of two parts pride, one-part regret churned through her.

The Café wasn't a shrine to her father, and yet she felt as though she was rearranging the very flowers on his grave. Was it okay for her to do that? To put her own mark on the place? Throwing caution to the wind and watching it swirl like the emotions tornadoing within her, Scarlett decided in that moment to allow herself the freedom to own the Café and its future.

Memories couldn't pay the bills, no matter how priceless they were to her.

Things needed to change and she was finally willing to lay the first stone in what she hoped was their path to success. She couldn't wait to take the next step.

THE HOUR HAND ON THE CLOCK HADN'T EVEN reached nine and she'd already made as many phone calls. She was going to need a larger shelf. So far, everyone she'd spoken with was on board. There would be jellies and preserves, spices and rubs, even coffee mugs with the restaurant's logo on them, supplied by the town's local potter. If she couldn't make it to the farmers' market weekly, the next best thing was to bring just a portion of that to the Café.

"What's got you smiling?"

Her back was to him, her face to the mostly bare display case, but the fact that her joy radiated that fully only strengthened her resolve in her decision. Ready to throw her arms over his shoulders in a celebratory hug, Scarlett whirled around and almost toppled completely over. Her hip caught the side of an empty chair. She grabbed hold of it as an anchor. Every other part of her came untethered, though, including the words that flitted right out of her brain.

"Scarlett?" Miles' head dipped under hers. "You okay?"

Blinking over to the woman at his back, Scarlett looked around the room for some understudy to feed her a line. Nothing came.

"Scarlett?"

The woman wasn't looking at her. Her gaze was angled toward Cooper, her hand curled around his. There was everything familiar about the way she interacted with the boy, like she had a place in his life that couldn't be challenged.

Insecurity as thick as a coastal fog blanketed Scarlett. She wanted to throw it over her head and hide beneath it.

"Miles." She finally said it with all the uncertainty of a person reading off a nametag at a meet-and-greet. "How are you?"

"I'm great."

He looked it, a man utterly pleased with his life and his lot. Whatever void the absence of this woman had created before was suddenly filled with joy unbound.

Could Lana finally coming around change him that much? Scarlett knew Miles had wanted the woman to acknowledge her son. Wanted a complete family for the boy, whatever that actually meant. The temporary part Scarlett had played had nothing on the peace this woman brought them. Cooper had been a happy kid before, but now he was content, the scattered pieces of his world finally snapped into place.

The walls of the Café squeezed in closer.

"Give me a moment?" If Miles had answered, Scarlett didn't hear it, the distance already marring his reply and the fuzzy whoosh of lightheadedness muddling his words. She lifted the counter hatch and let it slam down behind her.

The cooler. That might stave off the redness forming on her cheeks, might keep the humiliating flush from clawing its way up her neck and face. She bee-lined for the walk-in. Retreating to some refrigerated cave wasn't rational, but none of the actions she'd taken within the span of the last three minutes were. Might as well add to the rapidly growing tally of crazy.

Inside the cooler, Scarlett slumped against a wire rack, her hands catching a shelf ledge to steady herself. Breaths puffed in and out through trembling lips. One, two. Then three and four. Maybe her heart and her lungs weren't so erratic now, but her thoughts gladly took over in that area.

Hope nosedived within her like a kite without a tail.

Last night had been wonderful. Things often were with Miles. But the life he clearly had outside of Harmony Ridge had suddenly confronted Scarlett in the form of a beautiful brunette standing smack-dab in the middle of the Café. She was a physical reminder that Scarlett didn't truly know Miles, didn't know him apart from this adventure that she just so happened to intersect.

Why had she let herself fall for a wanderer? That's what he was, right? A man wandering through his life, searching for himself?

She'd thought he'd just been looking for a place to crash land, but there was always more to it than that. Fresh starts were appealing on paper, but when it came down to the nitty-gritty of starting over, hitching yourself back to the past was always the easier option.

It's why alcoholics went back to the bottle. Comfort in familiarity, even if it wasn't good for you.

Truth be told, Scarlett could use a stiff drink

herself right about now. Her eyes scanned the walk-in fridge, her gaze coming up woefully empty in that department. Who was she kidding? It wasn't a good idea to chase her worries away with bottom shelf booze. She needed to be chasing other things. Dreams. Success. There was an entire list of opportunity on the horizon for her. So what if Miles was no longer a line item in that?

She raised both shoulders with another cold inhale. She wasn't going to run. Wasn't going to hide. Harmonys faced life head-on. They didn't cower in cooler closets made for packaged meats and dairy products. With the determination passed down from her father, she reached for the handle at the same moment Dominic must've grasped the other side. Her body flung into the open kitchen, her cheek colliding with his solid wall of a chest.

"Scarlett?" Dominic looked down his nose at the woman sandwiched to him. "What the heck are you doing in there?"

"Oh." She sauntered backward and slung her thumbs into her belt loops, waggling her shoulders to her ears. "You know. Just doing some reorganizing."

Of her heart. Of her mind.

"Right." He didn't believe her. Clearly. Rather than play along, he combatted her obvious avoidance head on. "Miles is out there."

"Is he really?" Acting every part the ignorant fool, she moved around her chef to peer into the Café through the big pass-through window. "I had no idea."

"Uh-huh." Disbelief quirked up a corner of his broad mouth. "Why don't you go back in there and grab me the smoked gouda?" Scarlett nodded, following direction. "And while you're at it, snag some courage and nerve too."

Scarlett emerged with the wedge of cheese in question, but couldn't locate that bravery Dominic hinted at. It was nowhere to be found. Certainly not within her.

"He likes you, Scarlett." Dominic transferred the block of cheese from one palm to the other. "But you must already know that."

"It's—"

"If you say complicated, I'm going to wallop you upside the head with this hunk of artisan cheese." Might not be a bad idea. She could use some sense knocked into her and supposed a fancy gouda was as good a catalyst as any. "Of course, it's complicated, Scar. But that's never stopped you in the past. Just because something is complicated, it doesn't mean it's not worth *un*complicating. Some people are worth it."

She wasn't sure how to do that. How to separate the wheat from the chaff in this situation. Miles and Cooper, they certainly were worth it. It was her dang feelings that need to be removed from it all. And how was she supposed to do that? How could she let go?

Maybe by first realizing the role she wanted in his life had already been filled.

"Go out there," Dominic prodded, edging that darn cheese block in her direction.

"Okay, okay." Fear needled through her. "I'm going. But not because you told me to. Because I have other tables I need to check on."

She let the lie settle in her absence and pushed her way back into the main dining room. Miles, Cooper, and the mystery woman took up the corner booth, the one that seemed to be his favorite. He'd become a regular both in the Café and in Scarlett's heart without even trying. Maybe it was time to do some rearranging.

Hands clamped to her thighs, she strode to the table.

"Miles, Cooper." Scarlett rooted her feet in place so they didn't take off running. "Lana."

The woman nose-sprayed her soda clear across the table. "Lana?"

"You're not…?" Words not only failed her, but apparently her overactive imagination had entirely betrayed her too.

"I'm not Lana?" Stretching across the table to blot the mess from Miles' shirt, the woman slid a look over her shoulder at Scarlett. "No, definitely not."

"Scarlett." Laughing, tears slipped down Miles' face and into a smile that made Scarlett want to be sopped up and tossed away with that used napkin. "Have you ever even seen a picture of the band?"

"Sure, I have." Two sets of disbelieving eyes blinked up at her. "Okay, maybe I haven't."

"Lana is a number one, up-and-coming female country artist." The woman discarded the napkin on the table. "I'm—"

Revelation locked into place. "Maddie!"

"Yes." Miles' sister breathed a laugh. "I'm Maddie."

"And I'm completely humiliated." Scarlett dished out a look of apology, but she figured it got lost under the sheer mortification that scrunched up her face. "I'm so sorry. I don't even know why I assumed you would be Lana. I can't believe I jumped to that conclusion. You must think I'm crazy."

"No apologies." Maddie wasn't having any of Scarlett's groveling, thankfully. "And I don't think you're crazy. Not at all. I mean, I assume Miles hasn't really mentioned much about me either, since he hasn't told me anything about you."

Embarrassment passed the baton off to absolute disappointment. "Oh." A flush of heat burned the apples of Scarlett's cheeks. "Believe it or not, he's actually told me a lot about you. Which is why it's even more ridiculous that I didn't put two and two together." She smacked her palm to her head and made a face.

Scarlett tried not to lose hold of her composure, but was pretty sure her dignity, self-respect, and remaining shred of pride just got swept away by the busboy tidying up their table.

"Anyway." Scarlett took an unsteady backward step. "I'll leave you three to your breakfast."

Evidently, the fact that their table was right in the middle of being cleared wasn't a big enough clue that they'd already finished their meal. Just how long had Scarlett been in that silly fridge?

"I mean, enjoy paying your bill," she corrected, supplying the only thing she could think of left for them to do. "Okay. I'm just gonna go."

Hightailing it to the kitchen faster than fresh gossip spreading through a church potluck, Scarlett made her quick escape.

Miles caught her by the elbow.

"Hey." His eyes were filled with the mercy she couldn't give herself. "I'm so sorry about all of that back there."

"You don't need to be sorry, Miles. You didn't say more than two words. I, on the other hand, babbled enough incoherent nonsense for all of us."

"That's why I'm sorry. That I didn't say anything." His fingers grazed down her arm on the way to clasp his hands in front of him. "I'm sorry I didn't say anything to my sister about you, Scarlett. But I want you to know there's a reason for that."

"It's fine. Seriously. And to be honest, I don't really have time to chat about it right now, Miles. I have tables I need to get to." She pulled together her last ounce of fortitude to get the words out. "Maybe later?"

"Yeah." His head lifted in a gentle nod. "Later is good. Can I come by your place tonight?"

"Of course." Chin up, Scarlett forced some poise

into her voice and said, "But for now, just enjoy the time you have with your sister. Don't give me a second thought."

"It's sort of impossible not to give you a second thought, Scarlett." A flirtatious grin lacking any sort of subtlety paraded across his frustratingly handsome face. "And a third. And a fourth."

"Well, I've certainly given you a lot of ammunition today. Feel free to enjoy a hearty laugh at my expense."

"I'm not laughing at you, Scarlett." His eyes pleaded more than his words. "I'm serious. I don't want you to think me not telling my sister about us is any reflection of how I feel about you. Quite the opposite, actually."

She repeated with all the monotony of reciting the daily special. "I really don't have time right now, Miles."

"I know. You're working. I'm sorry." He slid back a foot on the checkered tile. "But I'll see you tonight. We can talk then."

Her mouth finally followed instructions and smiled. "And I'll be looking forward to it."

If dreading and looking forward to something were the same thing.

"Me too." He hesitated, then caught her gaze. "I'm really glad Maddie finally got to meet you, Scarlett."

"Oh, I'm not so sure that first impression was a very good one."

"I don't know." He shrugged. "Maybe not your best, but it was pretty memorable."

Stomach souring, Scarlett gave a false grin and turned toward the kitchen of the Café, worried that someday soon that's all she would be in Miles' life too. Only a memory.

CHAPTER TWENTY-FIVE

*M*addie's arms pinwheeled in wide circles at her shoulders. "If I push him on that swing any longer, these just might fall off!" She dropped her hands to her sides and shook them out, then lowered onto the space next to Miles on the park bench.

"He doesn't even let me push him anymore, so the fact that he's begging you to just shows how much he's missed you, Maddie."

"The feeling is mutual. But as I recall, I'm not the one who left town."

That comment socked Miles straight in the gut.

Why did it have to be worded that way: *leaving*? He knew a departure was necessary in order to arrive at the place he needed to be, both in location and in life. But the reminder that he'd left Nashville, left the band, left his only remaining family—that didn't sit well with him. Never had.

"I'm sorry. It's not fair for me to keep bringing that up." Maddie had been a mind reader even before she donned that psychic costume—complete with shiny crystal ball—back in the seventh grade. She always could discern her brother's unspoken thoughts. "I've just really missed you. Cooper too."

"And we've missed you."

"But it looks like you're finding your place here." She offered him the approval he'd silently sought since he'd taken that first turn off the highway toward Harmony Lane. "This town suits you, Miles. I can see why you like it here so much."

"Scarlett is—"

"One of the most endearing women I've ever met." Maddie's hand cupped her brother's knee affectionately.

"She really is. I'm not sure why she was so out of sorts today. She's usually not that scattered."

"I get it. I mean, if the guy I was in love with showed up with the woman I thought was the estranged mother of his child, I think I would've reacted the same way."

Miles tried that sobering perspective on for size and his mouth turned dry at the enormity of it all.

Did Scarlett honestly believe that if Lana had come waltzing into town, Miles would even dare to bring her to the Café as a party of three? Had he really been that unclear about their situation?

It struck him that maybe he had. If Scarlett had any reason for feeling insecure, it was Miles' doing.

He swallowed the depressing thought behind a swig of coffee from his cardboard cup and breathed out. "I've got some things I need to work out. Some things I need to explain to Scarlett."

Up in the distance, Cooper spiraled down a corkscrew slide. When he shot into the sand at the end of the run, his body collided with the legs of a young girl about his age. Half rising from the bench to untangle the disoriented children, Miles paused, his chest expanding with pride when Cooper popped up, shook himself off, and reached a hand down to pull the little girl to her feet.

"He's an incredible kid, Miles." Maddie took in the sweet scene. "And I know I give you a hard time for taking off, but I do agree that it's the best for both of you. Especially now."

The comment snagged Miles' attention, and his brows shot to his hairline. "What do you mean, 'especially now'?"

"The song."

"The one Lana stole from me that's practically gone viral? I've already heard it."

"So you know?"

"That she's using my material illegally? Yeah, I know. And I could probably hire an attorney and take her to court, but I honestly don't have it in me to battle her anymore. Legally or otherwise."

"Miles."

He'd never heard his name spoken in the way

Maddie uttered it just now, like it was a warning label for what she was about to say.

"Miles," she murmured again, at the same time her hand slipped into her purse to retrieve her cell phone. She swiped to unlock the screen and then passed it off to her brother. "Did you read the comments?"

"'Congratulating' her on her newest release?" He hooked his fingers in the air, making quotes around his words. "I saw those."

"They aren't congratulating her on the song, Miles." Maddie nudged closer. "They're congratulating her on her pregnancy."

His lap caught the phone as it tumbled through his fingers. He didn't need to spend any time calculating things. Of course, it wasn't his. But that didn't change the fact that he was involved at the very center of it all.

His throat closed around the words. "Lana's pregnant?"

"She is." Maddie's mouth went slack with empathy.

An incredulous laugh parted his lips. "That's the song I wrote when I found out we were pregnant with Cooper." The thought of Lana reusing it as some sort of birth announcement would've taken Miles out at the knees had he been standing. He slumped down further on the bench, his head hitting the iron back.

"She actually came by my place looking for you."

"She did? Why would she do that?"

"Because she's planning to raise this child, Miles. Said she's changed, and she's ready to be a mother now. And it will be Cooper's half brother or sister. She felt like you should know."

He ran a thumb along his clenched jaw, wondering how his back molars hadn't cracked in two. "What am I supposed to do with all of that?"

"I don't know. I really don't."

It wasn't as if he hadn't pictured a sibling in Cooper's future. Of course he had. Miles just figured he would be the one to give that to his son. When he thought of Cooper's family tree expanding, it never crossed his mind that it would branch off in Lana's direction.

"She doesn't have any legal rights to Cooper, Miles. She knows that. The courts made that clear. So this doesn't even have to be a thing."

Miles looked his sister in the eye. "Can you imagine if we weren't in each other's lives? You're all I have, Maddie. You and Coop. How can I take his chance at having a little brother or sister away from him?"

"It's not taking if it was never given to begin with. The ball is in your court here."

Was it? Because it sure felt like he had no say, no real options.

"That's why you came all the way out here."

Maddie looked on at the playground, but her gaze didn't latch onto anything in particular. "I figured you would need your big sister by your side when you heard the news."

He did. Family was everything. How could Miles deny his son that?

"So Cooper's going to be a big brother?" He tried to release a good portion of his frustration with an exhale, but there was still more inside of him. Wrapping around his head. Gripping his lungs. Breaking his heart.

Maddie switched her focus back to her brother. "Only if you allow him to be one."

CHAPTER TWENTY-SIX

*S*he knew he was coming, and yet when Scarlett saw the headlights round the corner and shine into her front room window on his way to park in her driveway, it was as though those two beams pierced right into her. Exposing her. Shining a light on all of her insecurities. Blinding her completely.

She owed Miles another apology, but Scarlett wasn't sure he would even take it. She might have come across as acting silly earlier that afternoon, but it didn't mask the real fact that her faulty assumption exposed something about her. Something about how much she trusted—or didn't trust—Miles' intentions.

She waited behind the door a beat after his knock to collect herself, then drew it open. "Hi, Miles."

He lifted and swung a bag bearing the logo of her favorite Chinese restaurant between them. "I brought dinner. I hope you haven't already eaten."

She hadn't, but that had a little something to do with the fear that whatever she put into her stomach might not stay there. Nerves had tumbled and twisted her insides more fiercely than a washing machine on the spin cycle.

"I haven't eaten yet. That smells delicious." She backed up to allow him entry. "Thank you for bringing it. That was really thoughtful."

He'd been in her house before, and yet she felt as if she were leading him through a museum.

"This is the couch where I've spent the last hour overanalyzing all of my crazy actions from today. And over here is the kitchen where I stared into an open fridge for fifteen minutes, trying to decide if I could stomach any of the options within it. And that phone right there? It's the one where I read and then reread your text about twenty times, seeing if I'd missed anything unspoken between the lines."

Of course, she didn't say any of that. She didn't say anything, really, and the silent wedge between them was even more awkward than if she'd confessed her inner thoughts.

"You can get things set up in here." She motioned toward the round dining table in the small nook off the kitchen. "I'll grab us some utensils."

"Not necessary." He brandished two sets of chopsticks in red paper sleeves. "Got all we need."

She'd wanted to hide, wanted a moment to collect herself, but she just smiled and joined him. She needed to stop treating townhome kitchens and walk-in coolers as save havens. She wanted to allow Miles the opportunity to prove he could be that for her instead.

Scarlett heaped large portions from each cardboard box onto her plate. When there wasn't a sliver of space left, she fretted with the chopsticks, tangling them in her fingers that suddenly forgot how to work.

"I can grab you a fork if that would be easier," Miles offered, his chair already scooted out halfway.

"Believe it or not, I usually do know how to use these." Building emotion surrendered to acceptance and she let out the breath suffocating her. "I'm sorry, Miles. I'm not acting like myself. I haven't really all day and I know you picked up on that."

"Scarlett, it's okay. Honestly. You don't need to explain. I realize seeing me with Maddie threw you for a loop. I should have given you a heads up."

"It did throw me, but that doesn't excuse my behavior. Even if it *had* been Lana with you and Cooper today, I should have respected your decision to bring her and left you all alone."

He hadn't tucked his chair back in just yet, and when Miles lowered his chopsticks to the edge of his plate and sat back, Scarlett mustered another breath, unsure what was coming. "Scarlett, I need you to know that things with Lana ended years ago. Before Cooper was even born, really. And if, for some reason, she did show up in Harmony Ridge, I wouldn't be having family meals out and about with her. I'm not even sure I'd let her near Cooper at this point. We're not like that."

"I know. You've given me every confidence to believe that, Miles. That's why I feel so dumb about my interaction with Maddie today. That two-and-two was so easy to put together, a kindergartener could've done it. You guys have a striking family resemblance."

His mouth raised in a forgiving smile. "You need to stop beating yourself up about the whole thing. Maddie really likes you."

"Not sure I gave her a whole lot to like."

"Of course you did. And Cooper and I gave her even more." He stretched his hands out in a silent request for hers. "I hadn't told my sister about you because the entire reason I left Nashville was due to a woman. I didn't want her to think my motivation for settling down here was because of one too."

The way his words strung together made sense, but her heart wasn't as easily convinced as her brain. Scarlett wanted to be the reason for his hanging around Harmony Ridge as much as she didn't. It was a big responsibility that carried with it their entire futures.

"You believe me when I say there's nothing going on with Lana, right?" Miles dipped his head under hers and leaned forward, elbows pressed into his knees. "I need to know that you understand that."

"I do understand. And of course I believe you, Miles. You've given me no reason not to."

Strength faded from his eyes. Releasing her hands from his, he gripped his hair and a groan rose to his throat. "I don't know any other way to say this than to just come out with it."

Scarlett could hardly breathe.

"Lana's pregnant." A single hand lifted and flew into the space between them like a crossing guard stopping traffic. "It's not mine. That's not even possible. But it doesn't change the fact that this child will be Cooper's sibling."

Hope left Scarlett in the tears that brimmed her eyes. Quickly, she shoved a hand to her cheekbones, but they came back damp. "Wow."

"I know."

She hadn't expected Miles' eyes to match hers. Something a lot like fear claimed his expression and his throat bobbed with a constricted swallow.

"I don't know what to do with this, Scarlett," he admitted. "I know it's unfair to dump all of this on you, but I needed someone to talk to."

She wanted to be that for him. Be a sounding board and a confidante. But this scenario felt like it came from an entirely different script than the one they had been living. She didn't know how to edit this news in.

"You can talk to me about anything, Miles. I hope you know that."

"I do. Even in the short time I've known you, you've become the person in my life that I want to tell first when something good happens. The flip side of that is that you get the bad news too."

"This isn't bad news."

Like the comment had caught him in the chest, he coughed. "What?"

"It's not bad news. A child never is."

A single tear curved down his stubbly cheek and under his jaw. He jammed his palm to his chin and sniffed. "You are amazing, Scarlett."

"I wouldn't go that far—"

"I am going that far and then some. You are an incredible, selfless, and caring woman. I came over here to tell you that my ex is pregnant and you somehow find the blessing in it. A blessing in the midst of all the ways this makes life more complicated. For me. For Cooper. For us."

"I was reminded today that just because something is complicated, it doesn't mean you should give up on it. Some people are worth sticking it out for. And you and Cooper?" An honest smile crossed her mouth. "I'll stick things out with you for as long as you'll let me."

Any other words Scarlett planned to say stalled in her throat. Miles twined her fingers into his, calling her from her chair into his lap. She easily followed and looped her arms around his neck as his hands found her back to guide her close. Foreheads touching, he murmured in a voice she almost couldn't hear, "I've completely fallen for you, Scarlett."

A vulnerable smile met Scarlett's lips before Miles' were on them. The kiss swelled with all the emotion of a country love song—that soft, sweet intro giving way to a lyrical confession of joy and hope. Carefree bliss. She knew it all by heart.

She'd fallen for Miles too, every part and piece of him.

He kissed her with an urgency he hadn't granted himself until now. And Scarlett knew it was that confidence she'd given him—a safe place for his worries and fears to land—that allowed it. She had never wanted to be that source of strength for anyone before, but with Miles, it was an innate pull that couldn't go ignored.

And this must be what love is, she thought to herself.

The threat of a perfectly good dinner growing cold was the only thing to ultimately draw them out of one another's arms. They talked all through their meal, mostly about Cooper, a little about Miles' new job down at the high school. And they didn't bring up the situation with Lana again. They had time to figure that out. For now, Scarlett was just thankful for the chance to be the one to help Miles process it all.

CHAPTER TWENTY-SEVEN

*E*ven with a full night separating the memory of his evening with Scarlett, the grin attached to his mouth wouldn't budge. It felt like a permanent fixture. And, just when he didn't think it could get any bigger, a vision up in the distance caused that goofy smile to expand ear to ear.

Miles let his foot off the gas and the vehicle decelerated to a crawl just as it came up to the county courthouse. If he'd had sunglasses on, he would've raised them, a hat on, he would've lifted the brim. All he could do was blink in rapid succession, clearing away any doubt over what his gaze took in.

Miles idled the truck along the curb and reached over the seat to roll the window down.

"Eugene? Buddy, is that you?"

His older friend turned on a polished loafer, swinging the woman at his side decked in wedding-day white around with him.

"Eugene, did you just—?"

"Marry the most beautiful woman in Harmony Ridge?" A weathered hand affectionately patted the forearm of the bride linking his elbow. He nudged back her lace veil and pressed a kiss to her overly rouged cheek. "You bet your bottom dollar I did."

"You sneaky little Casanova."

He shrugged. "Some days, you just wake up and think, today is a good day to start the rest of my life with the woman I love."

If truer words had ever been spoken, Miles had yet to hear them.

"Congratulations, my friend. I couldn't be happier for you."

"You're coming to the Café tonight to celebrate." It wasn't a question—not even a request—but an assertion. "Bring the little tyke and that sister of yours too. I want all of my family there." The man winked, then shuffled off with his new bride, leaving Miles sitting in the truck with that perpetual grin locked in place.

HE WONDERED WHAT SHE WOULD THINK WHEN SHE saw his caller I.D. pop up on the screen. Would she reciprocate his many acts of avoidance and send him straight to voicemail? He almost hoped she would, but then this game of phone tag would play out even longer. He couldn't run forever.

With a deep breath and a quick prayer, Miles punched the call button.

"Are you okay?" Lana's voice met his ear loudly, evidently no need for a *hello* or *hi*.

"Am I okay?

"Yes," she spat. "After falling off the face of the Earth. Must've hurt pretty bad."

The inward groan made his lungs tight as he strained to keep it contained. "Lana, we need to talk."

"Yes, we do." She added no more to it than that, just waited in silence for Miles to get the ball rolling. Okay, so this was how things were going to go.

"I saw the video," he said. "With my song."

"Nice. So you're one of the two point four million who liked it."

"Didn't say I liked it, just that I saw it."

He could hear the huff through the phone. "I figured you wouldn't mind if I borrowed it."

"I wouldn't call it borrowing. You stole it, Lana. Plain and simple."

"Just like you stole Cooper!"

Miles pulled in a searing breath through his nostrils to temper his mounting frustration. "I didn't steal Cooper—"

"You took off with my son! Didn't even bother telling me where you were going. Or that you were going anywhere to begin with! You don't call that stealing?"

"He's not your son, Lana." Maybe by blood, but not in any of the ways that counted, the least of those being legal. "You never showed any interest in him when he was around. Why the overnight change? Why do you suddenly care now and never back then?" He swallowed around the ball clogging his throat. "Is it because you're pregnant?"

Her voice fell to a whisper. "I'm not pregnant."

There were times when he couldn't stand the woman—despised her even—but he didn't wish loss on her. Miles' heart sank to his stomach. "Oh, Lana. I'm so sorry."

"Nothing to be sorry about. Wasn't pregnant to begin with."

"What?"

"I wasn't pregnant, Miles. Thought I was for a hot second there, since I had a huge craving for mint-chocolate-chip. Remember when I could eat a pint at a time when I was preggers with Cooper? I had a whole freezer full of those ice cream cartons."

Miles didn't need a mirror to confirm his jaw had dropped to the floor. He snapped it shut. "You're telling me you announced a pregnancy to the entire world without confirming it first?"

"Did you see what it did for publicity? My follows are through the roof. Timber Rose is trending on the charts again too. Not too shabby, if you ask me."

Yet another one of her stunts. He couldn't believe it, and yet her history of libel and lies had given him every reason to.

"Like I said, I thought I was pregnant for a

moment there. No harm in sharing the exciting news."

The woman had no clue about the amount of harm she'd caused in other's lives. This was just the tip of the very convoluted, very manipulative iceberg.

"Lana. I don't even know what to say to that."

"Nothing to say. And nothing to *sing*, I might add." Her voice grew heavy with irritation. "I get that you wanted out of the band, Miles. Fine. You're a guitar player. You can be replaced. In fact, you already have. But that whole songwriting thing we were doing together? That we were in the middle of? That makes things a little more complicated."

He waited for her to say more, knowing she wasn't finished. She never was.

"I don't have any *music*, Miles." The words were staccato, each one punctuated with anger. "And I'm supposed to head back into the studio next month. I've got nothing. Nada. Zip."

"Nashville is full of talented songwriters."

"But none of them know our sound. Our style. You can't teach that in a month."

"What are you asking here, Lana?"

"That you sell me your catalog." She didn't mince words. "No sense in you hanging on to perfectly good songs when you have no intention of ever using them."

It was the only thing she'd said throughout their conversation that made any sort of sense. And yet releasing his catalog—the songs written from places of both pain and joy deep within him—felt like handing over an intimate part of himself he knew she didn't deserve.

"Think about it, Miles. We'll offer what's fair. I'll finally get what's mine and then you won't hear from me again," she said, clearly more interested in the pieces of music than she ever was in her biological son. "That's a promise."

CHAPTER TWENTY-EIGHT

*C*hloe Loveland-Harmony moved her hand across the large hanging chalkboard sign, dotting the last 'i' with a satisfied grin. What typically broadcasted menu items and daily specials now announced the sweetest news of all: the union of Eugene and Lottie through a sudden—but not altogether surprising—wedding.

"That looks perfect, Chloe." Scarlett appraised her friend's precise handiwork. "They are going to love it."

"And hopefully they will love this too." Without taking his eyes off of the three-tier cake in his hands, Levi took delicately measured steps toward the Café's counter, as though balancing an overfilled fishbowl in his grip. "It's not my finest piping work, but on short notice, it was the best I could do."

Scarlett gripped her twin's shoulder. "If it has sugar and chocolate, it'll be perfect."

"It's got lots of both, so we should be good to go."

It had been all hands on deck and then some for the last hour. Even though Eugene had specified that they didn't want anything special—friends and family were all that they truly needed surrounding them—a wedding was a joyous cause for celebration. And celebrations involved food, drinks, flowers…all the festive trimmings.

Dominic and Timmy put together the most delectable charcuterie board that took up the entirety of the long bar, full of cheeses, salamis, fruits, and nuts. Chloe's brother, Brooks, came by with a case of wine from his friend's local winery. Beth, the innkeeper, provided fragrant lavender bouquets, all harvested from the garden in the back of the property. And Chloe penned sweet sayings of enduring love on colorful cardstock squares used for centerpieces on each café table.

And, of course, a wedding reception wasn't complete without music. It just so happened that Scarlett knew a gifted musician, one who gladly accepted the invitation to pull out his guitar and provide the soundtrack for the celebratory evening.

Thirty minutes after everything had been set in place, the glowing bride and groom arrived with all the fanfare of a walk down the red carpet at the Oscars. Scarlett loved that Lottie was still outfitted in her gorgeous white gown and hadn't changed into something more sensible for the reception.

"I feel like a princess in this," Lottie had confessed

through a giggle when Scarlett commented on the beautiful dress. "I just might wear it every day!"

There was something in that statement that caught Scarlett by the heart and squeezed it tight. She wanted that too—to do more of what made her happy, even if it seemed crazy on the outside.

Halfway into the evening, she located her chef in the small crowd and pulled Dominic aside. "Do you have a quick minute to chat?"

The man had been dancing up a storm and the sweat clinging to his brow rivaled the sheen he often wore when working in the hot kitchen over the industrial stove. "I've always got a minute for you, Scarlett. What's up?"

His feet kept two-stepping, while his arms moved rhythmically close to his body.

"I want to go a different direction with the Café, but only if you're onboard."

"As long as you don't want to turn the place into a cat café, you know I'm in. Totally allergic, otherwise I'd be all for it."

Scarlett's brow quirked at the oddly specific thought. "Nope, not a cat café. More like a pay-what-you-can café."

Dominic pulled a napkin from the dispenser on the bar and ran it over his face, still shimmying to the beat. "Isn't that sort of what we already are? Unintentionally, I suppose."

"Kind of. But I want it to be official. Rebranding and all of that."

Miles hadn't stopped strumming his guitar, but Dominic lost his groove for a moment and stood stock-still. "Scarlett…"

"We can make it work, Dom. I promise."

"The numbers aren't there. Yesterday was our worst day yet."

"I know. But doing this is me wearing a wedding dress everyday just because it makes me happy."

Dominic's mouth notched up on one side. "Yeah. I have no idea what that means."

"It means that I know this doesn't make sense— that it will seem crazy to everyone else—but this is what I have to do. This is what the Café needs to be."

"You know I'm onboard with whatever you want to do with this place, Scar. Even if that means going down on this ship with you if it all goes under."

She took her friend's bulky hands into her own. "It's not going to, Dom. We'll stay afloat. Promise."

The chef gave her an *I believe in you* grin, the one she'd seen his father give hers so many times over the years. "I've got some dancing to do, but let's talk about this more tomorrow."

"You got it."

Dominic twirled her around twice, sending her spinning into the arms of another man.

"Well, this is a treat." Eugene's hands found Scarlett's back and pulled her into a dance maneuver guys half his age would have difficultly keeping up with. Over the course of the evening, Miles' soothing guitar playing had morphed into something straight out of a country jamboree, and Eugene didn't miss a beat. Thankfully, Scarlett had had the forethought to move the dining tables to the outskirts of the room, creating a makeshift dance floor in the center of the restaurant. And with Eugene feeling this particular song, they took up the entirety of it.

"And with that, I'm going to take five," Miles said into the microphone when the lively song came to a close. He slipped off the barstool and cracked open a water bottle, bringing it to his lips.

Out of breath and with feet never more grateful for rest, Scarlett thanked the lucky groom and made her way over to Miles.

"You're doing great." She pulled another water out of the cooler next to him.

"So are you." He tipped his bottle toward the dance floor. "I didn't know you had those moves in you."

"Neither did I!" A laugh bounced between them. "Eugene's a dancing machine! I've never seen him this happy and full of life."

"Love will do that to you."

Off-balance from the comment and overheated by the dance, Scarlett pressed the bottle to her cheek. The condensation cooled her temperature down, but did nothing to squelch the heat flaming her cheeks for an entirely different reason.

Miles hadn't said I love you—not even close—but the word settled between them like an elephant plopping down in the middle of the room. They both ignored it.

"You sure know how to throw a party," Miles redirected.

"What's the saying? Many hands make light work? There's a bit of that going on here."

"I think there's always a bit of that going on in Harmony Ridge. It's one of the things I like so much about this place."

Just then, Cooper came barreling into Miles' legs, nearly taking him out like a bowling ball leveling a pin. "Daddy! Daddy!" He had Orson in a headlock under his tiny arm. "Pearl says our sunflowers are German!"

"Germinating," Pearl corrected. She sidled up beside the boy and rested a hand on his shoulder.

"It means they're starting to grow," Cooper supplied with a smile. "She said they're going to be even taller than me someday!"

"Might even get taller than your daddy."

"That's so tall!" Cooper squealed.

"Not as tall as that roof we installed the other day." Walking up with a glass of punch in his hand, J.P. eyed Miles over the rim. "Now *that* was tall. Wasn't it, Miles?"

"Hey, hey." Miles pressed his hands into the empty space. "We don't need to bring that up."

"What happens at the community garden stays at the community garden?" J.P. lifted just one brow and cocked his lips in a grin.

"Luckily, it doesn't," Pearl interjected. "Nothing stays. It all goes to the food bank and the women's shelter. Not a single crop left behind."

"I wish I had access to those delicious fruits and vegetables of yours, Pearl. You have the greenest thumb of anyone in this town."

"It's not hard to grow when you've got the space and the time."

"Both of which I have woefully little of." Scarlett's gaze popped over the top of Pearl's head toward the counter where Eugene and Lottie stood with a pie server locked between their hands. "Looks like they're about to cut the cake. And I don't know about you, but I, for one, am glad it's not a 'what happens at the bakery, stays at the bakery' sort of situation."

"Sugar is meant to be shared," Scarlett's brother, Levi, said as they ushered the group toward the impressive cake. "And if I do say so myself, this one is worth every bite."

LATER THAT EVENING, IN THE KITCHEN OF Scarlett's townhome, Miles folded the cardboard flap on the cake box that Eugene and Lottie insisted they take with them, and he stacked the leftovers inside the fridge next to an expired carton of almond milk Scarlett kept meaning to throw out. He turned toward her, his palms splayed on the island countertop between them. "There's somewhere I'd like to take you. A place I'd like to show you."

"Tonight?"

"It's a little dark tonight, but I'm thinking maybe tomorrow afternoon. Only if it's not too much trouble for you to miss an hour or so of work."

"I can do that. Believe it or not, I'm actually over-staffed tomorrow, so I should be able to sneak out."

With the confidence from the beautiful evening full of love and promise to bolster her, Scarlett slid around the island and placed her hands flat upon Miles' chest. Trusting blue eyes peered down at her through dark lashes, and he met her halfway in a kiss that had her fingers trailing down his shirt to grip the bottom hem. The slight rumble from Miles' throat unhinged her knees.

She loved this man. Loved the way he made her feel both respected and desired simultaneously. Loved the way he cared about the people most important to him. Loved his vulnerability—a trait many men seemed to think had gone out of style.

It had been a chance right turn off a two-lane highway that no doubt drove Miles straight into Scarlett's life and into her arms. She had never been more thankful for hungry stomachs and an open café that led Miles and Cooper there.

He pulled back enough to catch a breath, and ran a knuckle down the slope of her cheek and jaw. He caught her chin between two fingers and kissed her tenderly once more.

"I never want to leave."

"I think Cooper might miss you," she quipped before one more quick kiss.

Miles laughed. "I have a feeling he's enjoying his one-on-one time with his Aunt Maddie." The slow sigh conveyed his defeat. "But it's been a long night with the reception and everything. I should go. You just make it really hard to."

Scarlett slid him a look loaded with flirtation. "I know you should, but I wish you didn't have to leave."

"That's sort of the plan. To never leave Harmony Ridge. To never leave you."

That hope had been unspoken until now. But it was hinted at in the year-long contract at the high school and there in the way he looked adoringly at Scarlett like he'd never have eyes for another woman. Miles was laying seeds, planting roots, and settling into a life in the small town.

Scarlett couldn't wait to watch it all grow.

CHAPTER TWENTY-NINE

The towing company pulled up in front of the Inn just after dawn. Miles always figured he'd never see that trailer again. A big part of him even hoped he never would. But now, it no longer represented late nights, long roads, and packed tour calendars. Now, it was a vehicle for an entirely different dream.

Before Maddie and Cooper were even awake, Miles had hitched it to his truck, taking the back roads to avoid Harmony Ridge Row and too many eyes with too many questions.

He wasn't leaving town. Quite the opposite.

The cab of his truck had illuminated with golden rays as the sun continued its climb above the ridge. He felt that warmth in his bones, felt the gentle swath of light like a hug of affirmation.

When was the last time he'd let himself hope for a real home like this? It certainly never existed in the childhood that housed more pain than any young child should experience. His sister had done all she could to build him a shelter made of sweet memories and sacrifice, but Miles knew she'd been searching for that place of comfort too.

Tragically, Miles' mother hadn't lived long enough to give him that, and his father hadn't been out of jail long enough to call anywhere home but a ten by ten cell.

Things would be different for Cooper. Of that, Miles was certain. The signed escrow check—written with funds he'd just received for the sale of his entire music catalog—was the first step in making that happen.

"Did you know Eugene and Lottie were getting married yesterday?" Miles asked when he picked Scarlett up that afternoon.

A grin teeming with suspicion crossed her mouth. "I didn't until he called to ask about holding the reception at the Café. But I wasn't at all surprised. Just last week, he was trying to figure out how to tell her he loved her. I figure marrying her should do the trick." Her laugh stopped short. "You know? This officially goes down as Harmony Ridge's biggest grand gesture. And there have been some pretty epic ones."

Those words created a competition for Miles just waiting in the wings.

He understood Eugene's urgency, though. When you finally figured out what you wanted in life, it made no sense to drag your feet. The days were too few, the moments too fleeting.

With Scarlett pressed against his side on the bench seat of his truck, Miles drove out to the land he'd fallen in love with almost as quickly as he had the beautiful blonde next to him. It had room for Cooper to grow and space for their lives to unfurl. It would take time to get the rundown farmhouse in livable condition, but that wasn't enough for Miles to shy away from paying cash for the property on the spot.

Over the years, he'd gotten good at envisioning potential. He did it with music every day, starting out with those first few chords, adding layers of melody, and finishing it out with words that turned the song into something greater than all of its parts combined. He could do the same with the house. It had good bones and character. And with a little paint, love, and patience, it could become a home greater than any Miles had ever let himself dream about.

"Are you taking me to Flying R Ranch?" Scarlett peered past her knees toward the pink sneakers adorning her feet. "I didn't bring my boots and I'm not one-hundred percent sure they'll even let me ride after a truly unfortunate bucking bronco episode I had there back when I was twelve."

"This sounds like a story I want to hear. But no, I'm not taking you to the ranch." *Just past it on the right*, he wanted to add, but that would be a dead giveaway. "Should I start calling you Saddle Up Scarlett?"

"Definitely not. I think that was the entire problem. I didn't even have a saddle to begin with. Just hopped up on that cute-as-a-button pony, dug my heels into her sides, and took off."

"So that's not how it's done?"

"Not unless you want to get tossed into a creek bed and spend the better part of your Sunday afternoon picking burrs out of your backside."

Miles tried to shield the growing smile behind some form of stoicism, but all efforts came up empty. His smile burst as wide as his laugh was loud. "I'm sorry, Scarlett. But that sounds like it has all the makings of a pretty memorable weekend. I'm in."

She punched her fist into his side playfully. "I'd rather make memories with you that don't involve me being utterly humiliated. We already have more of those than we need."

"I'm not going to limit our memory making options. I want a whole bunch of them. All kinds."

Flipping the blinker signal on his truck, Miles began the slow turn down the long driveway. Split redwood fencing flanked them, guide rails toward a future he couldn't wait to start.

"This is the old Peterson's property," she acknowledged in a voice scarcely louder than a hush.

"You know it?"

She sat forward and clasped her elbows as she leaned toward the dash, eyes narrowed with nostalgia. "There used to be an old stone fruit orchard in the back. My dad worked summers here when he was a teenager. It's actually where he and my mom met."

"The trees are still there. They need a good pruning and some water, but the realtor said they're viable."

"Realtor?" Scarlett's eyes went as wide as the peaches she spoke of. "When did you talk to a realtor?"

"Last week when I put an offer in on the place."

Scarlett fell back against the seat at the same moment the truck rocked to a stop in a dirt road rut. "Miles...do you...?"

"Own this place?" His words wandered out in place of hers. "I do. Or I will, once escrow closes."

"This place has fallen in and out of escrow over the years more times than I can count. Sold and gone back on the market, over and over." Her jaw went slack, eyes still round with disbelief.

"There's evidence of that in the house. Renovations that appear to have started and stopped multiple times. The realtor said no one has had the energy to see it through. But if there's one thing I know I can do, it's see something to fruition."

The never-ending tour schedule he had to fulfill before his official exit from the band. The endless nights of rocking and soothing a sleepless child. The twenty-six-year journey toward a perfect moment, just like the one he currently found himself in.

"What's that?" Finger lifting, she pointed past the house.

"The thing I wanted to show you."

He left the truck first and found her hand to pull

her down on the other side. Her fingers closed around his. The ground was dry, dirt clods meeting the toes of their shoes with each step. It wasn't pretty and he could see why potential buyers might shy away from such a project, but that didn't deter Miles. This was his blank page; his empty stanza. The music would come and Scarlett would be his harmony.

"This was my makeshift tour bus when we were out on the road." He pulled hard on the handle, knowing the door often stuck in the jamb. "In here, it was just me and Cooper. It was the closest to home we ever got. But now, home feels a whole lot closer." He moved to loop his arms around her waist. "This is where I'll be staying until the house is ready. It's the best of both worlds—a familiar space in a brand new place. My hope is that it will make the transition easier for Cooper. I sort of had a hard time with this trailer and all it represented, but it was Cooper's first and only home. Once the house is done, I figure I can rent it out for a ranch hand or something like that. But these wheels have officially stopped in Harmony Ridge, and they won't be rolling anywhere else."

Her cheek moved to his chest, and her words pressed into his heart when she said, "We're not just a stop on a bigger adventure anymore?"

"You *are* my adventure, Scarlett."

He felt a puff of air feather along his neck. "It's sort of funny, you know?"

"What is?"

"Your name."

Chin tucked back, he said with a laugh, "You think so? This is the first I've heard of that."

"Not funny in the comical sense. But fitting, I suppose. You had to travel all these 'miles' to finally find your place. It's symbolic. I like it."

The symbolism didn't stop there. He released her and moved inside the trailer, coming out with a tote in his grip. "This is for you."

"You didn't need to get me anything."

"Just a little something I put together. It's a gardening basket, complete with everything you'll ever need."

Her eyebrows formed the question mark her words failed to. "Ever need for what?"

"To start your very own garden to grow all the produce you can imagine for the Café," he said. "I've talked a lot about digging roots and settling down. I want you to be right by my side as I do it, Scarlett. One shovel at a time."

"You're trying to rival Eugene for epic, grand gestures, aren't you?"

A vulnerable smile passed over his mouth. "How am I doing?"

Her lips on his served as the only answer he would ever need.

EPILOGUE

"*H*ow was everyone's first day of school?"

Cooper flung his lunchbox onto the bar and climbed onto the empty stool in front of him, winching himself up with legs dangling and kicking for momentum.

"Great! I already made five friends." He counted them out on his fingers and settled into his seat, popping up his index finger on the other hand. "No. Six friends!"

"That's amazing, buddy." Scarlett leaned on her elbows and turned her gaze toward Miles. Rather than a lunch sack, he lifted his guitar case to the counter to lower it there. "And what about you, Mr. Callahan?"

"I only broke two strings, called three kids by the wrong name, and lost four guitar picks. I'm counting that as a win."

"Well, I think both of your days are deserving of a cookie."

"Are we going to Levi's?" Cooper practically wobbled right off of his chair with excitement.

"We are, and you're going to stay there and hang out with him for a bit while your daddy and I head out to the property. Would that be okay?"

"Yup." Smacking his mouth, Cooper grumbled, "It's boring there. Just dirt and construction."

"And Waylon!" Miles said, reminding him that their friend, J.P., had adopted the dog and often brought him out to the farmhouse when working on the renovations there.

"You'll have to give him a hug for me." Both Scarlett and Miles giggled at that.

"Will do, buddy." He roughed his hand over his son's unruly hair. "Will do."

———

THE CAFÉ HAD HISTORICALLY BEEN SCARLETT'S favorite spot in Harmony Ridge, but Miles' property was trailing close behind. Everyday something new took place, from irrigation installation to garden box building to soil tilling. While Miles had hired J.P. as a contractor to handle all the tasks associated with the farmhouse remodel, Miles and Scarlett tackled the garden related projects with gusto and the knowledge they'd gained from internet research and Pearl's graciously imparted wisdom.

That hand trowel Miles gifted Scarlett had already proven its worth, and the blisters on her hands told the story of countless evenings spent with their fingers deep in the soil, the sunset as their backdrop, and the sounds of construction from the farmhouse their hope for the future.

"What are we planting today, Farmer Miles?" Scarlett withdrew her gardening tote from the bed of his truck and fell in step as they covered the ground toward the gardens.

"Not sure I'm worthy of that label just yet. We'll have to see how many of these plants actually grow."

"They'll grow," Scarlett assured him, slinking her arm into the crook of his elbow.

He turned his head and pressed a quick kiss on her cheek. "We're planting sunflowers. I figure we can get one last harvest in before Thanksgiving if we plant soon. Don't you think those would look pretty in the Café?"

She knew they would. In fact, she was grateful for anything this land could provide. Already, just their small summer crop had offset much of the Café's usual produce costs. This property was the gift that kept on giving, feeding, and nurturing, and it was as much a blessing to her as the man at her side.

The rebranded Café was only three months in, but the pay-what-you-can concept was in full swing, and the numbers climbed steadily. It had helped that they'd figured out the source of all those dwindling dollars. Turned out Katie had been their secret spokeswoman for free meals, often telling guests it was 'on the house' even before taking their orders. She'd admitted that once, as a young girl, Jack Harmony had gifted her family a complimentary meal and that very act was the main reason she'd applied to work at the Café in the first place. She recalled the over-whelming sense of gratitude about the offer, and the joy it brought to Jack to so freely give it.

"That, and people complain a lot less when their meals are already free," Katie had also admitted.

In any other restaurant, it would be a fireable offense, but that lean toward generosity was some-thing Scarlett valued in an employee. Sure, it needed to be shaped and molded, but Katie was teachable and worth the little trouble it would take to get her there.

Plus, now that they had a true system to allow others to pay for and donate meals in the form of a bulletin board with *Give-One* and *Get-One* meal tags, the whole operation moved in a much smoother—and more sustainable—fashion.

For Scarlett, everything had fallen into place in both life and love, and she couldn't be more thankful.

In the garden, she settled in next to Miles, their hands working in unison to dig out tiny tunnels to drop the sunflower seeds into. A small portable speaker provided the soundtrack for their work. They often listened to music while they labored. It had surprised her one day when Miles even suggested they turn on the latest from Timber Rose. Over the months, he had come to terms with his decision to sell his repertoire of songs to Lana, but it still stunned Scarlett that he would actually want to listen to them.

"I always thought I would be the one to play these," he'd confessed one afternoon when their elbows were deep in the dirt and their conversation had turned to things more serious. "Turns out they sound every bit as good coming from someone else's mouth. Maybe it's not the song that really even matters. Maybe it's all about the person singing it."

Scarlett had challenged him on that. There were so many parts to making music—just like there were so many parts to running the Café. Her dad had been the one to compose the original piece, but Scarlett was the musician currently playing it. It was a blended effort, but a beautiful harmony all the same.

"I'm going to go grab another packet of seeds." Miles nudged his head toward the planter box in front of them. "You want to take over this row while I run to the truck real quick?"

"Sure thing." Scarlett kept up her steady rhythm, plunging her finger into the soft dirt to create space, dropping a seed into the ground, and patting the soil firmly to cover it all up. It was assembly-line work, but she still found joy in each and every seed she planted.

Miles jogged back moments later and passed off an opened bag of seeds. "Here. Why don't you start on these?"

"Teddy Bear sunflowers?" She had never heard of the variety and took time to study the picture of the fuzzy, golden-yellow bloom on the packet. "Well, isn't that absolutely adorable and completely fitting?" She shook the sachet out, her breath altogether leaving her when something else entirely plunked into her palm.

"Scarlett."

Whipping her head around, she met that deep-sea blue gaze she'd fallen into that first day at the Café. "Miles." She stayed crouched down at his level.

His lips lifted into a humorous grin, and he took the ring from her shaky grasp. "Would you actually mind standing for this?"

"Oh, of course." She popped to her feet, all wobbly, with a heart that beat like a kick drum within her chest.

"Thank you," he said sweetly, still lowered to one knee. "Scarlett, last spring, when I met you, I wasn't looking for love. I was just looking for a meal and a few nights in a town that would welcome a traveling stranger."

She pushed a single tear from her cheek.

"Love was the furthest thing from my mind. But somehow you pulled it out of me—you managed to pull out what little hope I had left of ever finding someone to share my life with. Someone to share *our* lives with."

On cue, Cooper came bounding out from behind the trailer, previously tucked out of sight. Both Chloe and Levi suddenly stepped into view, but remained on the periphery while Cooper rushed forward and pummeled straight into Scarlett's legs. She gathered him into her arms, hoisting the boy close and squeezing him tight.

"Scarlett." Miles drew her attention back down. "Nothing would make us happier than to have you in our lives forever. To grow with. To learn from. And to continue this great adventure as a family, together. Will you marry me?" Collecting her hand, he hovered the gorgeous solitaire diamond inches from her finger. "Will you marry us?"

"Of course, I will." Her knees crashed to the ground, Cooper's arms still wrapped around her neck and legs around her waist. "Yes!"

Releasing his grasp, Cooper shot back across the yard toward Levi and Chloe to relay the answer, and the couple thrust their thumbs high into the air in congratulations, a hoot and holler accompanying the gesture.

"I love you, Scarlett." Miles slid the engagement ring onto her finger, then lifted her hand and pressed his mouth to that same spot. "Falling in love with you has been my heart's greatest detour, and now it's ready to stay put. Forever, here with you."

She tossed her arms around his neck and kissed him with all she had—all the hope for their future, joy for the present, and thankfulness for the choices that drove them from their pasts and straight into one another's arms.

THE END

KEEP READING!

For a BONUS chapter from Scarlett and Miles' love story, join Megan's Newsletter here:
https://bit.ly/3wG5lUh

Follow J.P. and Nora's story in ***In Sweet Harmony***, book two in the Harmony Ridge series. Available for pre-order now!

Nora Paisley's life is sweet. She just launched her local honey label and sales are taking off. It's the success she needs to prove her beekeeping dreams are worth pursuing, something her ex-boyfriend continually challenged her on. But even though her hives are thriving, her recent heartbreak isn't easily forgotten.

As a contractor, J.P. Weatherford is good at building things. He spends his days renovating dream homes for his clients, but the one thing he can't construct is a life that brings fulfillment. It doesn't help that he was left at the altar when his fiancé decided his older brother was an upgrade. J.P. knows he's rough around the edges. He just hasn't met the right woman to smooth out his sharp ways.

Lately, the bees buzzing around his job site aren't helping his mood. And the stubborn beekeeper who won't remove her hives from the nearby property is starting to get under his skin.

Nora's frustrated too. J.P.'s music is too loud, his personality too cross. And when their names are drawn to partner for the Harmony Ridge summer festival, the last thing she wants is to spend time with the bristly man next door.

Can two adversaries reconcile and come together for town tradition's sake? Or will stubborn wills and the sting of past heartbreaks keep them from discovering a potential love swarming right around them?

Also by Megan Squires

A Lake House Holiday

Join Megan Squires' Reader Group!
Join my corner of Facebook where I share sneak peeks, host giveaways, and get to know my readers even better!

To stay up to date on new releases, please sign up for Megan's newsletter:

http://subscribe.megansquiresauthor.com

ABOUT THE AUTHOR

 Growing up with only a lizard for a pet, Megan Squires now makes up for it by caring for the nearly sixty animals on her twelve-acre flower farm in Northern California. A UC Davis graduate, Megan worked in the political non-profit realm prior to becoming a stay-at-home mom. She then spent nearly ten years as an award winning photographer, with her work published in magazines such as Professional Photographer and Click.

In 2012, her creativity took a turn when she wrote and published her first young adult novel. Megan is both traditionally and self-published. She can't go a day without Jesus, her family and farm animals, and a large McDonald's Diet Coke.

To keep up with Megan online, please visit:

Made in the USA
Coppell, TX
02 April 2022

75917265R10156